Published by Ad Hoc Fiction.
www.AdHocFiction.com

Purchasing Information:
Paperback available from www.AdHocFiction.com
E-book available from all usual outlets.

Printed in the United Kingdom.
First Printing 2021.

ISBN paperback 978-1-912095-02-5
ISBN e-Book 978-1-912095-01-8

the other side of better

by

Michelle Elvy

AdHoc Fiction

for my mother

Here, with Michelle Elvy's *the other side of better*, are wise reflections cast through refracted light. Here is the scent of the sea, the rift and grit of childhood. Here is an absorbing cinematic poetry in the telling – breathtakingly honest and elegant stories (personal, yet universal) about how we live, how we struggle and, most enduringly, how we thrive. A wondrous collection!

–Robert Scotellaro, author of *What Are the Chances?*;
co-editor of *New Micro: Exceptionally Short Fiction*

Michelle Elvy needs no more than this, the smallest white spaces in which to swim the waters between story and poem with humour, colour, imagination and a sharp grace. Elvy watches and listens to her characters, and the places they dance in, bringing us the darkly joyous truth of life's uncertainties and love's ambiguities.

–Tania Hershman, author of *and what if we were all allowed to disappear* and *How High Did She Fly?*

the other side of better teems with innovative, intimate adventures, each a microcosm of humanity made capacious through Michelle Elvy's sharp, unique lens.

–Christopher Allen, Editor of *SmokeLong Quarterly*

Well-turned stories, rich with wit and detail, that explore the spaces between people and places, from the 'concrete weight' of history to the secrets of creeks, islands and oceans.

–Paula Morris, author of *False River* and co-author of *Shining Land: Looking for Robin Hyde*

The poems and stories in *the other side of better* hopscotch gingerly between wanderlust and rootedness, desire and exhaustion, memories of reality and dreams of the impossible. This is how Elvy gets you, by luring you in with one wonder and then giving you another. And the trick is never the same twice. This is a collection that surprises not just because it can, but because it understands the surprises of the world.

–Erik Kennedy, author of *There's No Place Like the Internet in Springtime*

Modern, humane and pacy, Michelle Elvy's short-short stories alternately cause gut-leaps and heart-settlings. In lush prose, she deals equally skilfully with pain and rapture. *the other side of better* is a gorgeous collection about love, the environment, and the things that make people devour and deify each other.

–Nuala O'Connor, author of *NORA, Mother America* and *The Juno Charm*

Each of the tiny, knowing stories in Michelle Elvy's lyrical collection the *other side of better* bears vivid fruit, and its cumulative yield makes for a luscious experience.

–Ethel Rohan, author of *In the Event of Contact*

These unique stories of love and dreams and oceanic epiphanies could only come alive at the hand of Michelle Elvy. In *the other side of better*, Elvy showcases her considerable flash fiction prowess and flair for innovation. It is a delight to see how she plays with the form and bends it to her will.

–Kathy Fish, author of *Wild Life: Collected Works from 2003-2018*

Flash Fiction locates itself between poetry and prose and the stories in Michelle Elvy's *the other side of better* lean towards either pole as the content dictates, some pieces hauntingly poetic, some laugh-out-loud funny, yet others resonant, lingering long in the mind. Cleverly, Elvy uses the economy of the form to keep her powder dry. Often, the full implication – sometimes enormity – of the story is only realised after the reading is over.

–James Norcliffe, author of *Deadpan* and *Dark Days at the Oxygen Café*; editor of *Essential New Zealand Poetry*

Michelle Elvy creates a fiction that is honest in its refusal to be confined by arbitrary standards of expectations. Place is everywhere, life is universal, people are real. This is how her writing begins. The works in *the other side of better,* her stunning new collection, widen narrative constructs and content into different forms – always surprising, always engaging – as if the writing itself demands encounter. To read Elvy's work is to move closer to discovery – is to find a larger view of possibility.

–Sam Rasnake, author of *World within the World* and *Cinema Verité*

Contents

lost and found 1

Antarctica 3

A midsummer night's shore 5

The Wall: a love story, of sorts 6

And in the museum: triptych 8

Sled 10

The laugh that was always there 12

The model bakery 14

Fish forever 15

Treasure 17

Spin 18

The Fuddy-Duddy Editor Weighs In 20

Lost and found in Berlin 21

Lessons from childhood: the chair 29

Lessons from childhood: remedy 31

Harmony 33

Secret 35

Patent leather 37
Lessons from childhood: apples 38
Lessons from childhood: watermelon 39
Gallery 40
Love, story 42
Three houses. 44
The Fuddy-Duddy Editor Comments On Real Versus Imagined 45
North. 46
Birdy 48
What are you afraid of, Jeannie B? 50
The fantail and the blowfly, 1940 51
Jersey (not Józefów), 2010 (not 1942) 52
What we ate 53
Pencarrow, now and then. 54
Itch 57
Close your eyes 58
Impossible weather 59
X. 62
Roll the die 64
Wanderer 66
Morning flash 69

Idea for a long documentary film 70
The Fuddy-Duddy Editor Gets Real: Write Like You Write 71

The Fuddy-Duddy Editor Intrudes 73
The Fuddy-Duddy Editor Started Out As A Fuddy-Duddy Writer 75
The Fuddy-Duddy Writer Reflects On Her Fan(s) 77
The Fuddy-Duddy Writer Looks For Her Story 79
The Fuddy-Duddy Writer Explores Her Childhood: Dodge Ball 81
The Fuddy-Duddy Writer Explores Her Childhood: Swimming Pool 83
The Fuddy-Duddy Editor Goes To Berlin: And Then They Danced 85
The Fuddy-Duddy Editor Plays Scrabble...............87
The Fuddy-Duddy Writer Is Thinking Of Breaking Up With Her Fan 89
The Fuddy-Duddy Editor Dreams An Impossible Dream: Block Party....................90
The Fuddy-Duddy Editor Reflects On The Importance Of Oral Hygiene: You Say Arugula, I Say Lettuce....................92

The Fuddy-Duddy Editor Breaks Out of Her Comfort Zone: French Kiss 94
The Fuddy-Duddy Editor Knows Her Limits 96
The Fuddy-Duddy Editor In The New Year 97
The Fuddy-Duddy Editor Is Working On Her Memoir 100
The Fuddy-Duddy Editor Reflects On Love 101

in a dream in a dream in a dream 103
Time to rest 105
Elephant 106
Giraffe types a letter 108
Aquinas, acid and me 110
Longing 112
Juggler 114
How to make lolo 115
Black and white and grey 117
Snapper 118
Earl Grey 120
Up the creek 122
Sign language 124
Hippo talks shit 126

Nothing happens at sea 128
Paint 130
The Fuddy-Duddy Editor Nods In Agreement 132
The long way 133
New world 135
Latitude adjustment: arrival in Stewart Island 138
Tell me what you think 140
Escalation 141
A knobby thing 142
Whale shark 144

Acknowledgements 149
About the author 153
About the artist 154
About the artwork 155

lost and found

Antarctica

The man finds the boy in a drainpipe and when he asks him *what are you doing in there?* the boy looks at him as if he should already know and says *I'm looking for Antarctica.* At home, the man's wife catches him staring at the tiny specks of dust spiralling in the late-afternoon sun and when she asks *What are you thinking?* for about the millionth time he hates her but he also knows he'd hate it even more if she stopped asking so he shrugs and says *I'm thinking about Antarctica.*

He goes back the next day and the boy is gone. He waits for him because he knows there's something they needed to say but forgot. The sky is heavy metallic: the hour before snowfall. He pulls his collar tight and heads home and when he gets there his wife's standing naked in the kitchen. It has started to snow and the only colour in the room is the orange of her fingernails. The snow falls and they can't get warm, no matter how hard they make love. Later he's staring again and his wife says *Antarctica?* but how could she know he's more than a million miles away with the boy in the drainpipe.

He returns to the drainpipe and crouches down on his hands and knees. His shoulders barely fit but he wedges himself in. He is about to turn and crawl down the pipe, all the way to a new continent, when a stranger walks by and sees him and when he asks *what are you doing in there?* the man looks at the stranger as if he should already know.

A midsummer night's shore

Coasting, gently coasting. Our sailing skiff moves purposefully parallel to the shore. A sandbar juts out and canvas claps as we tack away. A heron wheeling low near shallows, to port. We tack again and you say *Going in closer*, and grin, Puck-like.

Sliding the skiff along mud bottom, we come to a gentle halt. Squishing feet, wet marsh. I feel the chill of a cooler west wind and wonder why we don't just stay a while on this safe shore but you snap your shot and click click, squish squish, you're suddenly finished and push off again. You stow your Canon, tack out and then we're gone. You're a man with a plan.

I look back and spy the heron. Still shadow and sorrow, offending no one and standing for everything. He lifts his slow wings and flies low and sure – wanderer of the night. My wants are a blue-grey ghost, gliding along mudflat, a taunt

too close to shore, too close to night.

Now, moonrise. Another sandy spit. We rub bottom.

The Wall: a love story, of sorts

for Cary and Sabine

You remember our first dance? You there, me here: a mismatched pair. You held out your hand. I didn't know you, but you pulled me up, up, up… and I let go of everything and found myself in the arms of a strangely familiar stranger. We were high, floating on a wild November night. Hot breath, cold sweat, embracing an orgy of frenzy, noise, delight. We marvelled at the night, argued about wrong and right. I drank your Coke, you smoked my F6.

Just like a commercial.

Five years later and we're making commercials, only this time it's Vita-Cola-Realpolitik and you keep saying *baby, we're selling what sells.* You and me and Ostalgie. Don't worry that the kid's crying; Mama and Papa are self-employed. *Achtung, baby,* you keep saying, like it means something. But you still haven't learned my language.

And now we don't fight about wrong and right but the bottom fucking line and Turks living upstairs and bicycles crowding the entryway of our apartment building. *I need to get in and out,* you say.

I'm sick of the Marlboro Man but I pull long and hard anyway and can't help but laugh when you come to bed wearing a stiff shit-green VoPo hat you call a relic, a *find*. But I feel a worry growing in my gut, wonder if our children will be more like *us* or *them*, and I realise what I really mean is whether they'll be more like *me* or *you*.

And in the museum: triptych

The triptych, left: a whaling boat, riding high on rough seas. The tail of the whale is wrapped in ropes, thrashing; the boat is a bobbing wooden toy. The curator points – *Class, listen* – and speaks of form and shading. Girls squirm and boys move in close. John shuffles forward and is pressed behind Marianne. He worries he smells of sweat. Beth, to Marianne's right, turns and glares. Beth is always at Marianne's side. They have matching sweaters. John is wedged in, trapped behind the girls. His arm brushes against Marianne's. Beth takes Marianne's hand: a barricade of laced fingers.

The triptych, right: whale beaten and beached, men standing triumphantly atop his back; meat has been sliced from the creature's body and laid out on the sand. John lowers his head and tries to move right, away from such close proximity to honey-scented hair, but now he is forced forward, between Beth and Marianne. The front of his trousers brush against their still clasped hands. Beth shoots him a mean look, cuts right through him.

The triptych, middle (the largest image): the boat alongside the great creature, the first harpoon stuck in firm, the harpoonist perched with second harpoon raised. Ready for the kill. The crewmen row to keep steady. The boat rides on frothy waves. A grotesque and dizzying moment. John's skin stings at the sight of the harpoon. The curator's rising voice – *Class, look!* – chills his spine. John is sweating profusely now, squished between Marianne's prickly sweater and Beth's cruel gaze. The curator's voice stabs into his head. He closes his eyes and rides the waves.

Sled

The world slumbers,   silent   breathing   waiting.

Moments held in branches black and ancient, white shoulders heavy with weight of winter. This tree holds us in her bent arms, her drifts like sand. She sifts time, whips wind. Catches my snowflake memories, almost lost, worn by years of forgetting, of playing adult.

One memory especially alive: fresh as snow, crystal clear. Red mittens, speeding sled, a split rail splitting, sled skidding. Too fast into everything: the fence, a gash – and cousin's cold fingers mending me warm, his breath in my hair, voice in my ear, whispering thaw as we toked up and drifted into snow.

snow
fire and snow
fire cousin and snow
fire-breathing cousin sled and snow
fire-breathing cousin sled bed and snow
sled snow and tea, cigarettes my cousin and me
fire snow cigarettes, drink my cousin with tea
cigarettes and tea and me buried in snow
cigarettes muffled memory and snow
cigarettes and snow
cigarettes

Memory melts but this snowdrift landscape shapes the scar on my head. Rub it, feel the fence still. Some days. Others, leave it alone. My sled in the shed, slanted under a tarp, out of sight. My mittens are blue, not red.

The laugh that was always there

When Henry Watson's 1980 Buick LeSabre skidded off the road, he expected to see his life pass before his eyes. They say that happens, the whole birth-to-this-minute flash. Instead, he saw only parts of it, some parts blocked for years, like when his daughter found him masturbating in the closet – he'd felt mortified, almost zipped himself; what he saw now, in the moment the LeSabre careened round the corner and dived into the muddy ditch, was not the look of disgust he'd assumed (which had covered *his* face) but something else entirely – amusement or possibly even understanding. The masturbating turned into blending malts in the kitchen with the lid left off: there was his wife in the corner, long before cancer ravaged her body, her mighty laugh exploding at the eggs on the ceiling and the malt powder on his chequered shirt, her soft hand caressing his unshaven face. There were other moments, too: a sudden and violent slap across the face of his three-year-old son which he'd regretted for thirty years, a blinding sunrise in Athens, a scowling man outside the shop where he purchased his coffee every morning for thirteen years, the white tail of a buck gambolling away yesterday as he lowered his Browning and didn't fire, a waterfall somewhere in upstate New York – roaring like his wife's mighty laugh, here again, too. The laugh that was always there, even as he lost sight of everything and the world went black.

The model bakery

While the rest of the world turned on its axis and went to war and declared peace and went to war again and declared peace again and eventually engaged a new kind of war, a war that would last generations and be final proof that we'd all gone mad, while the socialists and communists and fascists and capitalists and anarchists and pacifists and economists and existentialists and astrologists and ufologists and scientists and homeopathists and nanotechnologists and nihilists and objectivists and evolutionists and creationists and occupy-ists advanced theories on progress and history and movement and change and a better life and a worse life and the end of the world and the new age, as well as the benefits of vitamin C and the dangers of gluten, the baker in Palmerston North, like his father and grandfather before him, pulled the shutters up on a new day and hung the wooden sign in the window:

THE BREAD NEVER VARIES

Fish forever

Old Nick sits at the table, waiting. He waits a lot these days, though he's not sure what he's waiting for. His daughter Sarah arranges the place settings while kids run up and down the hall. Music is playing too-loud on the radio, by a too-loud band wearing too-loud clothes. Old Nick doesn't understand this music. He liked music back when he strummed banjo and ukulele with his mates Joe and Ben, playing old haunts near their kauri-swamp home: Awanui, Māhimaru, Paparore, Sweetwater.

"Actually, we were pretty good," says Old Nick to no one in particular. Old Nick is old.

"What's cookin'?" Bruce opens a can of beer for his father-in-law as his wife looks cross and says, "Fish pie." A smile crosses her father's unshaven face. He's wearing the same sweater he's worn for three days, the olive-green one with a wine stain on the front. *I must remember to mend that hole in the elbow*, Sarah thinks. She sets the casserole dish on the table and begins to cut into it. "Kids!" she hollers. "Eat!"

"What kind of fish?" asks Alice, the first to pull up a chair. Alice is fifteen, hair drawn over her eyes in the fashion of youth and a *Fish Forever* t-shirt slipped sloppily across her skinny shoulders. Sarah braces herself for the fast-food-overfishing-sustainability lecture she's about to get. Sarah buys hoki 'cause it's on sale. Every time she does it, she pledges it'll be the last time.

The other three kids crowd in, elbows and knees bumping awkwardly till they settle into their seats. Sarah serves. Tony, the youngest, says a quick prayer. They all *Amen* and tuck in.

Soon the noise of plates, cutlery and glassware overtakes the radio music. These are the blended sounds that hold Old Nick's family together.

Old Nick asks, "Snapper?"

"No, Papa," says Sarah.

"Lots of snapper," says Old Nick, and no one corrects him because they know he's drifted off someplace else.

Tonight he's in the swamp with his cousin Erik, seventy years back, rolling on kauri logs and fishing on the Kalkino Creek down on the Heath's old farm. They throw a net in, and come up full. They joke about Mary Jane and who will marry her. Erik says it'll be him but they both know her heart is already Nick's. They pull the net in again. In less than an hour they have more snapper than they can eat.

"One hour," Nick says, to no one in particular. "That's all it took."

His family looks at him like they always do, pass the dishes around once more.

Old Nick chews slowly, says, "Fish's good."

Treasure

When Jackie and Jim first rolled around in the sack, they were teens, mere beginners. All limbs and movement, no tact or grace. It didn't matter, of course: enthusiasm and energy made up for lack of finesse. One night Jackie lay next to Jim, sweaty and heaving but confused. "There's got to be more to orgasm than this." Jim left the room quickly, returned with his mask and snorkel. "What the hell are you doing?" she said as he climbed up the foot of the bed with his snorkel gear dangling. "Free diving," he grinned, snapping the strap on his head. "Going in deep, looking for treasure." He found it alright, but it took a little roadmapping along the way. They spent years diving deep, snorkelling in the shallows. Learning how to breathe.

Ten years later, Jackie's holding her breath. Jim's gone and Ralph's down there looking for treasure. She's not sure he's ever gonna find it at the rate he's going. She considers asking him if he needs a GPS, bursts out laughing. Then the tears come and Ralph's out the door. It occurs to Jackie then and there that the years with Jim were good ones, real ones, even if in the end she needed more constancy, less finesse.

Spin

on a merry-go-round. An uncertain girl with a more certain boy who takes her hand and off they fly, hair streaming behind, blonde-brown-blonde blending billowing in a blur such a blur I cannot see them though I occasionally glimpse a wide white grin and hear laughter echo,   spinning   outward toward me   then fading

but the story neither begins nor ends there – I know because this is my story too and the end is clear, twisted in satin blue-ribbon fate, the ribbon which when pulled from her hair becomes the boy's undoing because once she says yes there is no turning back and she is his and he is hers   forever and so they say   and so they do

but that does not happen first. No, the story begins elsewhere entirely, in a field, the girl born to a dying mother, with the boy in a barn clearing hay and cobwebs from his weary eyes and hoping for a good day at the fair   which he has some fifteen years later when he meets the girl and pulls the ribbon from her hair and that day marks the   end-middle-beginning in a rush of colour   a rush of life   of death   of everything between

and I'm the between , lying in my golden field
waiting for my girl who will join me here once her story both
ordinary and extraordinary ravels its way to its end, ribboning
blue, and I wait and sing as we all wondrously and sometimes
recklessly but always constantly spin

The Fuddy-Duddy Editor Weighs In

The Fuddy-Duddy Editor notes:

1. Where is the ending to this story?
2. Shades of Shakespeare, puttering in the wake of greatness?
3. Too soon for a love story?
4. Careful not to tell too much.
5. We don't really care that much.
6. *Now* we care more: life in a flash.
7. Dry our tears with humour, but not too much.
8. Keeping it real – need more of this.
9. *For goodness' sakes!*
10. There must always be a beginning, middle and end, even if you pretend to not have one.

The Fuddy-Duddy Editor was once a Fuddy-Duddy Writer. Every now and then she glimpses herself in the lines of someone else's story, except with ~~incorrect~~ different moments of punctuation.

Lost and found in Berlin

for Werner and Gisela

1. City Center

You arrive in the city from far away. You've come by train, from the west. You've come to be a scholar, with little more than a winter jacket and a suitcase full of books. Great scholars breathed in this city. This was a place for philosophy, education, music, poetry. Still is, though some of the city is closed now. You've come to open doors and peek inside. It's your habit, this curiosity. Your work takes you back through time. Not to converse with poets and philosophers but to ask questions of men and women doing ordinary things. You're not interested in ideologues from the past. This is 1988. Politics carved the world in pieces that almost make sense. But you've got an inkling that the world is more than Us and Them. You've got your own set of questions. Some are harder than others.

Day after day you sit in musty archives and read letters of dead clerks of state, men who did nothing other than maintain books and keep things running. You like being alone with old correspondence, piecing together puzzles – words and meaning darting out of view like blackbirds flying off the page. It's your job to call them back, to line them up on the fence, one by one. To listen to them even when you don't like the *caw-caw* of their voice. This is how you connect the dots and write history. It's easy enough to do; you take one step at a time. Methodology matters when you are peering into someone else's life, when you are telling someone else' story. You dig deeper into the center of it all. You are a fine scholar.

These books, these letters, these words – this is all that matters.

2. The suburbs

One morning you take the S-Bahn south, all the way to the end of the green line. Lichtenrade. You have an address on a small scrap of paper, friends of friends. *Go have coffee,* they say. *You'll like these people.* So you travel an hour outside the city, heading away from your familiar musty world into a landscape green and packed neatly with rows of houses. You have never been this far outside the city; it seems like a different world altogether. You arrive at the house and knock. You are greeted by an old woman with gooseberry bushes in her garden and an old man with trains in his basement. They are story-book characters, she with plump cheeks and a smile you can't resist, he with an angular gait and a curious grey glint in his eye.

"Come in, have some cake," the old woman says. "We have berries and cream, too."

"Come to my basement," the old man says. "I'll show you my city."

You go to the basement first. Here you find a miniature city sprawling on a massive table made of several old doors. There are city blocks and recognisable monuments; there are parks and lakes. There is the Ku-damm, there is Alexanderplatz, and way off over there is the Wannsee. And there are trains – old trains and new trains, all on perfect tracks taking them in large circles around the old man's basement. Trains travelling impossible routes, crisscrossing the city center like they've not done in forty years. Where dark spaces exist in the world above, in this old man's basement a whole city breathes and lives, connected and electric.

"You see," says the old man, "This is *my* city. I once lived in this city where the trains ran like this," – he motions expansively – "from *here* to *here*."

3. The countryside

On the next visit, you watch the old woman pluck gooseberries in her garden. The bush is much higher than you expected, its prickly branches towering over her small frame. You reach to help and snag the back of your hand.

"Careful," the old woman says, and she takes your hand in hers. Her fingers are small with knobby knuckles, but strong. She gazes at your palms. You hope she's not about to tell you your future, but instead she says, "You don't go outside much, do you?"

When the berries have been collected, the old man says, "Come, let's go for a walk."

You follow them down a path leading out the back of their tidy garden. You arrive at a set of train tracks and the old man stops. He pulls a handkerchief from his breast pocket and wipes his brow.

"If you listen, you can still hear the trains," he says. His wife then takes his hand and leads him farther down the path. You go with them as they walk along the tracks. You follow as far as they go. This turns out to be not very far at all, because soon you come to a thick, weedy place, greened over fully but with rusty bits peering out in patches. You are in the countryside now. There is nothing around but empty space. A wildflower reaches out just on the edge of an abandoned field. Beyond, on the other side of the field, is a wall that cannot be climbed. In the evening the old man and the old woman tell you of a past you know from books: airstrikes and airlifts, hunger and hurried footsteps in broken streets. You feel very young next to them. You feel like you know nothing. You think about the dead men and their letters in the archives. You think about the story you are trying to write. You listen to the old man and the old woman and you hear their whole story in those tracks behind their garden.

4. Architecture

You visit the old man and the old woman many times. You must take the S-Bahn one hour from the city center and then walk another ten minutes to arrive at their house. You usually spend a whole day. More and more you think the dead men and their letters can wait. You need to hear these stories. You spend many autumn evenings in the garden, and when winter comes you sit at their kitchen table and sometimes you read in the basement while the old man tinkers with his trains – a new bridge here or a new tree there. You come to love the sour paint smell of his basement. You come to love gooseberry jam and peppery biscuits. And you come to know their early life, how they scoured piles of rubble for bricks for the house they would build, how they hand-polished each one, together. They tell you how they worked morning noon and night until they had built a proper house for their children. You think of the dead men's letters in the archives and how some of them may have died just as the first son of the old man and the old woman was born. You imagine the world then, decades back. The dead men, not dead yet but defeated and broken. This old man and woman, then quite young, building a new life brick by brick.

5. No man's land

You have been here more than a year when you wake to great commotion. People are running through the streets. There is a pounding on your door. It's your neighbour: "Come, we are running to the Wall." *Die Mauer.* It has become a fixture in your life – a place you bring your sister and brother when they visit, a place for graffiti and artwork. A place that inspires poetry in spite of itself, poetry read in dark cafés with tea lights on tables. Your neighbour rushes off, his footsteps gathering momentum as he rumbles down the stairs. You think this is a protest so you follow him, for you know you will not be able to sleep. What you don't know is that the whole city will wake up on this night.

You dance on the Wall – for days, for weeks, for months. People who never visited this city before arrive in droves. Relatives visit with heavy-duty suitcases. They carry large pieces of concrete away to set out in their shiny homes. "A piece of history," they say.

One cold winter day you take the train all the way south to the last stop and visit the old man and the old woman.

"Come, let's walk," says the old man, and he takes his wife's small hand in his. You follow them into the garden and out the back. You walk along the train tracks as far as they go, and this time when the tracks end you continue on through a patch of scrub and overgrowth. You keep walking, past the tracks and out into the open field. There is no sound but your crunching boots and the wind passing over the tops of stray weeds. Just beyond is a wall that could not be climbed.

"Listen," says the old man. "You hear that?" You cock your head; you hear nothing. "That is the sound I've been waiting for. Quiet. Peace. We are standing here. We are standing here and we do not have to leave. We can go this way, or that way. We can go forward, or back. Which way do you want to go?"

You are chilled to the bone. You are standing in no man's land. You do not answer.

The old man smiles with his grey eyes and takes your hand. "We will stand in this space as long as we like," he says. "This land is ours. It is *ours*."

6. Big City

In time, trains rumble behind the old couple's house again. Months have passed since you've visited. You have been reading and writing and understanding dead men's letters, and now you must leave. You travel on the S-Bahn once more to the end of the green line, this time to say farewell. When you arrive the coffee is on the table and the garden is abloom. It is May. You hug the old woman and step inside. It is dark in the house and the old man lies in bed. His breathing is shallow. The old woman leads you into his room, says, "Look who's come to see you."

"You've seen my new train?" he says.

You walk down the basement steps. You expect a new bridge, a new tree. You discover that the train has taken over the entire basement. It sprawls into rooms you've never seen. Old stations have new lights and new stations have been added.

Back upstairs, you say, "You've been busy." The old man smiles weakly. His grey eyes are grey.

"Your city is big," you say. He looks small in his bed. He takes your hand.

"Yes," he says. "My city is great. *Großartig*."

The S-Bahn rumbles past – so close you think it is crossing the back yard. The old man closes his eyes and sleeps.

Later, you board a train that carries you away from this city. You write stories from the dead men's letters. You become an accomplished scholar. You are very good with words and are invited to attend conferences and symposia. You lecture and tour and discuss the meaning of dead men and their letters. Time and again you are asked the same questions.

"You lived in Berlin? You lived there before the Wall came down?"

"Yes," you say. "Yes."

"Did you march on November 9? Did you dance with a *Vopo*? Did you collect pieces of the Wall?"

"Yes, yes," you say. "Yes."

But you can't tell them some things. You can't describe what it was like to feel the rumble in your chest when the train trundled down the track behind the old man's house once more. You can't capture what it was like to see the old man and the old woman smile in that grey field where nothing grew for forty years.

To stand in that space between lands and hold the old man's hand.

Lessons from childhood: the chair

"It's time to move the chair." I knew what Grandma meant: time to put the old green easy-chair on the curb, the one with the saggy seat and fraying arms, the one that smelled of oil and sweat and Old Spice and also old age and forbidden cigarette smoke. I knew it was time to take it away but dreaded it. That chair had been Grandpa's place in the house. I came home from school every day and found him sitting in his chair. After short happy days at primary school, I would climb into his lap and read him books about farm animals. In later years, I scratched my homework notes sitting cross-legged at the coffee table while he concentrated on crosswords. "Maisy, what's the world's tallest building?" he might ask. The chair was as constant in my life as Grandpa. Prom dates were cross-examined, college friends were greeted from it, occasionally asked, "Seven-letter word for hairy?" Once I was lectured about smoking from the chair, but I knew Grandpa occasionally snuck outside to grab a Pall Mall – I'd discovered his pack hidden in the coffee table drawer way back during my algebra years.

In the end, the hospital trips were dreadful, the funeral was bitter. But removing the green chair was my least favourite task. I rescued Grandpa's last pack of Pall Malls from the coffee table drawer, half-carried and half-pushed the chair across the front lawn, then sat in it till dark.

Lessons from childhood: remedy

It didn't surprise me when my dad moved out. It had been a long time coming. I had expected it, even wanted it. What surprised me was the scene I found when I came home from hockey practice that day. I walked through the kitchen door, saw Mum standing at the long kitchen counter, the one we climbed on as kids, the one we helped roll biscuits on. She held a meat mallet in one hand, tenderizing steaks for dinner. Across the room was Dad, leaning on the table drinking a Budweiser, looking as if nothing had happened (though his sweaty brow and shaky hand told me otherwise). And then there was my older brother Robbie, sitting on a chair in the middle of the room, his eye swelling yellow and green the size of a baseball. My mother looked up briefly. My brother appeared beaten (though his one good eye told me otherwise).

No one spoke.

What Dad did next was grab a steak off the counter – a thick juicy one that Mum had not yet pulverised – and place it on Robbie's eye. Almost gentle. "It'll help," he said as he made for the door. He glanced back once, not at my mother and not at me, but at Robbie, who half-shrugged, half-nodded.

My mother took the floppy Popeye-remedy from Robbie's eye, offered him a cold-pack and a dose of ibuprofen. Then she placed the steak on the counter and pounded it tender.

Harmony

She stands with her sisters, pretty maids in a row, feels cold despite the scorching spring sun. Words from the Lord fly around her head like the flighty trill of robins above; the birds make more sense. First handful of dirt: Mother.

She knows it is her turn next but cannot move, frozen by the burning house. Everything gone, ashes to dust to thousands of trickling mudslides when the cruel rain came the following day. Now, three days later, she feels the elements closing in: earth swallowing the dead, sky wailing a dirge, water washing ashes, flames singeing her heart. She laughs. Panic? Fear? Is the Lord's prayer funny? Or is it the preacher's (rubbery) voice, or the (absurdly) matching Franklin twins? The wide white collar (too wide, too white) on her cousin's velvet dress, her tightly wound curls? The acrid stench of spring, the crocus pushing up beside the blacked smudge that was their home? The father they just buried is gone forever (never mind what the preacher says)

burned up   swallowed down   washed away.

What she knows: everything will be drab without him (his smile, his reassuring voice, the way he danced with Mum in the kitchen with no music playing, how he let one of his daughters lead, always, when they biked the wooded path, how he tucked the sheets just right, all the way to her chin). What she doesn't know: four women will weave in and out of each other's lives for seventy years more, disconnected by geography but writing the same story in four parts, filled with all of it, with the memory of his voice, with sorrow and sound and colour.

Secret

The boy awaits the girl. He fidgets. He's planned everything just right. He wants the afternoon to be perfect. He has combed his hair and chosen his favourite t-shirt, the striped one. He recalls his mother saying it brings out his eyes. Whatever that means. But Mum's a girl so he reckons she knows something about what girls like. He has been thinking for a week about what girls like.

The girl shows up, a small blue bow on the left side of her hair. The boy thinks she's splendid, though he'd never say so. They play jacks, they play cards. Mum makes them lemonade, then says, "Jess has to stay for dinner, her parents are running late. You two go play in the garden a while. It's shady and cooler now."

The boy is glad. She's staying for dinner: it's practically like she's part of the family. He hopes Mum will ask him to set the table. He'll place her setting next to his.

The boy and the girl sit on the rusty garden swing. Time passes and he feels fine. He glances over at her to see how she feels, but he can't tell. She is smiling, so that is something. "You want to see my collection? It's secret," he says.

In his room he pulls the shoebox from under the bed. When he stands, he senses how the girl steps closer. His skin prickles. He places the shoebox on the floor and sits cross-legged in front of it. He looks up at the girl and sees a series of conspiratorial afternoons like this together. His heart pounds when she sits opposite him, the musty box between them.

He unwraps the contents, pulling old newspaper and tissue off as carefully as he can. In the bottom sit four small skulls. Dreadful eyes, large and oblong, drooping down. Noses flat and misshapen. Wide moaning mouths.

The girl gasps, leans in for a closer inspection. "Careful," he says. "They're haunted."

He showed this to his younger sister once, and she ran away screaming.

The girl reaches out a light finger to touch the top of one of the skulls. "Can I hold it?"

"Maybe next time."

At dinner, their secrets fill the space between them. He worries over his small deception. He wonders when he'll tell her that his skulls are only ripe seed pods. Antirrhinum from Mum's garden.

Maybe next time he'll tell her. Maybe next time he'll let her hold them.

Patent leather

You usually don't look past the sunshine face, moon mouth and neatly plaited hair. You usually don't look past the pastel Polly Flinders dress, turned down bobbi-socks and black patent-leather shoes.

You usually don't look.

And if you don't look, you miss the road map tracking the girl's nine-year life across this earth: the sharp outline of square shoulders under puffy sleeves, the hard jaw offsetting apple blossom cheeks, the always alert irises behind baby-doll lashes.

If you don't look, you might not see her at all.

And so, when the boy pushed the girl into the playground dirt one cold October morning, he could not have guessed what would happen next. He did not expect that she would gather her scattered books and pick herself up, rub away her snot and tears, and face him with a flash of fury and a precisely placed patent leather kick.

He hadn't yet learned how to read maps.

Lessons from childhood: apples

We carried Grandpa's useful truths in our sandy pockets and stacked them in the corners of our minds like rocks collected at the shore. Lessons like

Chocolate is delicious but sex is better

and

Miles Davis' Sketches of Spain will change your life

and

Your girl is always the best.

Eat the whole apple, to the core, he said. You'll live forever. I believed him when I was ten. He was living proof – died when he was onehundredandfour. We ate our apples with great care, my brother and me. Last year my kid brother died at thirty-three – a bitter rotten thing.

Maybe Grandpa was a liar after all.

~~~

"Pour me one, too," says Tracey, and we sit on a midnight porch with whisky and fireflies and the mournful meanderings of Miles Davis. I drink to my brother and know Grandpa didn't lie – he just got the one about apples wrong.
~~~

Lessons from childhood: watermelon

Old ornery, we call her: crazy, possessed, wild orange hair and wandering eye. Lives in the old wood shack. We guess she must've been there forever.

We play who can look the longest without blinking, coming home from school. Most days I wind up flinching and Warren wins.

But today I fall on the pavement, scrape my knee, *Hurry! Get home! Hurry!*

Salty tears, muddy hands, scared skinny me hobbling past her shack hurriedly.

But wait! She's waving now, evil eye glowing, frank and knowing.

Boy, where you going with that knee?

I want to hide as she beckons me inside. I feel fear clawing at my chest but her eye don't move away.

Mothball house, bandaged knee and not a word spoken. I learn her name. *Twila.* She cuts watermelon into small triangles. I nibble, then gobble. Delicious.

She does not scold me when the juice drips past my elbows, down, down, pooling on her polished wooden table. Not once.

Gallery

They went to the gallery together but when they stepped through the door their hands drifted apart and they meandered down separate corridors, and this is how they always went: travelling together along two paths. In market streets he'd seek gourmet coffees while she'd follow her nose to the smelliest cheeses; underwater, he'd linger near the colourful sunny surface while she'd dive into deeper blues and purples; on hikes he'd look for shady patches while she'd search out the sun.

Lately, he'd been wondering if she'd wander off one day. Now he found himself spying on her in the gallery.

The first time he found her, she stood in front of a portrait of an older woman. It was as if he'd intruded on a private conversation, so intense were their eyes peering into each other's.

The next time he found her, she was falling into an Escher-like ocean labyrinth. She tumbled down through spirals and space, and he wasn't sure he could get her back.

The last time he found her roaming off into the rolling hills of a distant landscape, her body so small in front, as if she were disappearing into the milky greens.

She turned and caught his eye, said, "Let's go home." Her smile opened up like the hills.

Love, story

I don't read fiction he said and it was such a profoundly ridiculous denial of something so essential like saying I don't breathe air or I don't make love or I don't like music forfuckssake that all I could think to say in response was I don't use commas.

I was determined of course not to like him but he swept me off my feet anyway with his long locks salty skin and an impossibly perfect pizza crust which he'd learned not from a Neapolitan *grandmama* but from a deliberate study of yeast and flour.

And for a while it worked. A shared love of pasta and seafood and cheap wine kept our minds off our differences. So too the other usual things: movies plays sex showers. But he didn't like King Missile and I didn't like ABBA even though I consented to seeing *Mamma Mia* with him one cold November night (the things you do in those early fuck-happy days).

We argued over religion and science and politics and it was fun.

Later we argued over religion and science and politics and went to bed sour and silent.

After I broke it off he used to call me.

He sang ABBA down the phone: *Take a chance on me.*

I sent him a copy of *Last Chance to See* (non-fiction after all) with a list of things extinct.

He wrote in an email: What happened to our love?

I wrote: It was fiction.

How could it have come to this? I'm living with insufficient punctuation and trying to break up with a man who doesn't believe in truth in fiction and models his love life on bubble gum pop.

~~~

I'm in a new relationship now. No Benny, no Björn. We curl into each other, like commas. We argue over religion and science and politics by day and go to bed with Ondaatje and Heym and Le Guin. We breathe air, make love and play music loud.
~~~

Three houses

for Marc

The first house I built was in the early 1990s. Pre-internet software engineering firm. *Boom!* went our stocks. Father *tsked* his tongue, muttered things like *house of cards* and *Icarus*. But I was pigheaded, grew the company fast and furiously. Invested in shiny black NeXTcubes, played DOOM till 5am with Marty and Jeff. I secured bank loans and spoke at California conferences with Steve Jobs, got a sprawling cherry desk with a view of Boston's harbour. Then a cold wind blew in, huffed and puffed and *kaboom!* went our stocks.

The next house I built was in 1999, a bonafide urban walk-up love nest. Stan and I moved in together within three months of meeting. Mother *tsked* her tongue, called it a house of fire. But I was pigheaded and didn't listen – and Stan was hot. Neighbours carrying groceries smiled at me in the stairwell. We drank wine and played chess at night, made love till dawn. Then a cold northerly blew in. Her name was Ilse. She huffed and puffed till he moved out. I licked my burnt ass and didn't call my mother for a month.

Then I built my third house. Both parents *tsked* their tongues, but said little. It's smaller than the others – more modest than the first, more secure than the second. And it can stand up to the wind. So when the cold northerly huffed and puffed this time, I hoisted my sails and went with it.

The Fuddy-Duddy Editor Comments On Real Versus Imagined

If you are going to write a story about your Younger Years, frame it in imaginative terms and embellish so as not to give the whole story away. There's mystery and freedom to Writing/ Being a Writer, and you have a lifetime of material to mine.

Be sure to eliminate the parts that ought to be labelled 'No One Cares'. First kiss? Ew. Throw it out. Love, told in a new way? Unlikely. Blows to your fragile ego? Welcome to the club.

But keep it brief and make some of it up – that's the only way to make your story interesting.

Ask yourself: what makes your story *your story*?

(Nice take on those three piggies.)

North

North is where everything is familiar. There is the wild terrain at the very tip of your island where the Pacific and Tasman meet: *Te Rerenga Wairua*, the leaping-off place of spirits, with clashing currents and male and female seas Rehua and Whitirēia bashing up against each other in noisy overlapping foam. There is the comforting smell and feel of the low beaches of the protected bays where you learnt as a boy to swim, to windsurf, to dig pipis and dive for sweet scallops. There is the memory of your father's hand, a hand that delivered blows across your backside and carved beauty into kauri. A hand that pulled you out of the water after you fell from the skiff one October day off Whangārei Heads and sank down through the deep while the blue got bluer and the light above grew further out of reach. There is a memory of your mother floating away on a warm wind when you were six, all of her flesh and blood and bone turned to dust and released to the sea and sky, sifting through your fingers at the water's edge. You sobbed with sorrow but also relief that she was not part of something called the *underworld*, but airborne now, floating with long white clouds out over the shimmery sea.

North is where you know every turn of State Highway 1 and every dune of the long western beach. North is where you named giant trees that had not yet been named by legend or the Department of Conservation or anyone else: sensible names like Milo and Willy Wonka. North is where you collected frogs and butterflies and snails and geckos. North is where you kissed your first girl but never saw snow. North is where the call of the morepork, back and forth, *ru ru*, announced the evening like clockwork: melancholic and predictable and soothing.

North is where you reckon you'll return, one day.

But today, you hitch your pack to your shoulder and shake your father's hand and walk across the threshold. You move slowly in predawn shadows. You walk down the path to the edge of the paddock and suddenly recall something else about his rough hand: the feel of it in yours – every day, for a time – on those silent morning walks to school after your mum was gone. Her soft ashes and bone specks caressing your palm, his fingers wrapping tight around yours.

You shut the outer gate and reach the road just as the sun crests over the hill to the east. A familiar autumn wind turns cold: a front sweeping in from the west.

You turn south.

Birdy

Young Kitty dreamed of Drake and Stanley, Nightingale and Joan of Arc. And when she first saw aeroplanes skimming along the harbour skies at Kohimarama Beach, she was spellbound. No ship or earthly vessel would contain her: she would take to the skies.

I want to fly, Daddy.

Daddy enrolled Daughter in music and dance but she flapped her arms to get airborne. Everyone laughed at the awkward girl, who shrugged and kept flapping.

I want to fly like Lindbergh and Hinkler. Please, Daddy.

Daddy rustled his newspaper and sank deep into his chair.

I want a Fokker tri-motor, Daddy. I want to fly across oceans, like Kingsford-Smith.

Sure you do, Kitten.

Daddy took her interest for flight of fancy. Daddy took her to a reception in Auckland, where the press welcomed Kingston-Smith from across the Tasman. Daddy shook Kingston-Smith's hand and introduced Daughter.

Now you've met him, Kitten.

Next year, Daughter got Mum to take her west, to Australia. Up she went in Kingston-Smith's old Fokker tri-motor. Southern Cross painted ribbons across the low-hanging heavens. There was no turning back: sell the piano, quit the music lessons. Daughter scrambled to London for flying lessons, crashing pluckily into fences and pastures but still believed.

Watch me kiss the sky.

Wings flapping, Birdy planned her first solo flight. Packed all the items on an essential check-list: cork sun helmet, food and water, first aid kit, ropes and torch, fishing line and hooks, magnifying glass, flint.

The press looked on. *But you're a girl, Kitten.*

She looked back. *Oh yes, so I am.*

She took with her a silk frock and a tropical flying suit. Eau de cologne, a powder compact, lipstick, too.

Now watch me go. And don't call me Kitten.

What are you afraid of, Jeannie B?

in memory of Margaret Cahill

I came to Te Hāpua as a young teacher. I was never scared, nor lonely. People back home in Wellington felt sorry for me, so far north, so far from home. I never minded – mail delivery arrived once a week and a radio connected us to the world, with a battery and an enormous aerial in the garden.

At 90 Mile Beach I was introduced to toheroas for the first time. I had never seen them before. I watched as people dug them up and put them back. Their little breathing holes everywhere on wet sand. Little lives just under the surface. Mere could eat the 'tongue' raw, straight from the sand. I saw her do it, and I did it, too. Later, my family said I was a cannibal. I'm not afraid of that.

Last week at 90 Mile Beach a boy drowned. Mere shut all the windows. Shut the house up dark and tight. *Because of the boy's kehua,* she whispered. Next day the villagers went to the beach looking for the boy's body. I would not go, I said. I could not see a dead body, I said. But Mere clicked her tongue, said they are more afraid of the spirit than a body lost in the surf. Passed me her woollen shawl and said, *Wrap it tight, there's a westerly blowing.*

The fantail and the blowfly, 1940

The Pied Fantail has shown up three days in a row. Mrs Morris can see it from the kitchen window. It comes at dinnertime, flits from branch to branch, then dives to the veranda and returns to its perch among the trees. A pīwakawaka. A messenger.

Mrs Morris makes soup. Supplies are scarce but she has onions and potatoes in the pantry. The fantail swoops again and plucks a blowfly out of mid-air. It's a large meal for such a small bird. She thinks of her boy, Elton. The last letter was weeks ago, when he was bound for Britain. He'd dreamed of flying since he was a kid. Now Europe seems impossibly far away. It will be getting cold there now, just as her veranda is warming in the October sun. She wonders if he's eating well, if he's getting enough sleep. She wonders if they have fantails there.

She dices an onion. Her eyes water. She wipes them on the corner of her apron. The fantail is battering the blowfly now. He lets it go and it flies away, staggering, slowing. The fantail swoops again, grabs it in its claws and pecks wildly. The fly is torn piece by piece. It crashes to the veranda and the bird dashes to swallow the now bite-sized morsels.

The fantail flies back to its branch. Mrs Morris shivers.

She dices a potato. Her eyes water. She wonders where her boy will be flying at Christmas.

Jersey (not Józefów), 2010 (not 1942)

When asked why he did it, the boy averts his eyes, fidgets. He does not lie, but he cannot face the truth. His lip trembles and he shakes when shown the photos. When asked to describe his role, he employs the passive voice and talks about others: *I was told... They insisted...* When pressed for an explanation, he refers to a chain of command: *I did what they said.* He talks about the older boys, the way he wanted to belong, the way he went along. When asked if he pulled the trigger, he nods and shrugs. When forced to talk about what really happened in the woods, he cries at the memory – the shallow grave, the waste of life. He did not want to shoot the dog, you can tell. There is no hate in his eyes, no fanatical glint. He is not accustomed to such cruelty. He is an ordinary boy.

What we ate

Honey

Honey, fish and toheroas

Honey, fish and toheroas, plus eels

Honey, fish, and toheroas, plus eels, and also ducks

Honey, fish, and toheroas, plus eels, and also ducks, and pheasants and hares

Honey, fish, and toheroas, plus eels, and also ducks, and pheasants and hares, and godwits

Honey, fish, and toheroas, plus eels, and also ducks, and pheasants and hares, and godwits and snipe

Honey, fish, and toheroas, plus eels, and also ducks, and pheasants and hares, and godwits and snipe, plus kūmara, spuds, corn and watermelon from Spirits Bay

Pencarrow, now and then

in honour of the Pencarrow lighthouse keeper 1859-1865, Mary Jane Bennett

for Kirk

I've climbed every lighthouse since you were lost.
Up and down, up and down. Up again and down.
Keep a sharp eye out, the expression goes.
Keep an eye out for ships, for storms,
for you.

Mary Jane's eyes search the night and she wonders
what her husband saw as the waves swallowed him
whole. The eye of God. The eye of the Devil.
The eyes of his children. The eyes of
his wife.

This storm has no eye, no calm: it lashes manic. I bend
myself towards the lighthouse. I am hunched, I am stabbing
into the wind – the wind so sure of itself. I brace
my body, fold in on myself. The wind blows
through   me, dries my skin, shrivels my
voice. It carves the hard face of these
cliffs, whistles metallic. There is
nothing   soft here,
nothing soft in
its dark hum.

Mary Jane polishes the lenses daily in her cast iron
tower. She touches the cold sure surface as she
descends the stairs: pieces pieced together to
save lives. The children's voices screech
manic across the wind. She wants to
gather them to her and hide them
under her skirts but they love the
wind   especially the youngest.
She is married to this headland,
to this dark hum.

I climb the lighthouse steps quickly, look out
to sea. I wonder if you know
I am watching.

She climbs the lighthouse steps quickly, looks out
to sea. She wonders if he knows
she is watching.

Itch

When the new girl Mary showed up in geography class, Ted felt his throat go dry. When she sat in the wooden chair next to him, cold sweat crept down his spine. And when she led him to the creek after school to show him how she caught frogs bare-handed, his heart soared. That night at dinner, he blushed when his dad mentioned the new girl, said something about knowing her uncle. He felt a red flush creep up around his ears and into his cheeks, but hoped Dad was too busy burning the steaks and Mum was too busy keeping his sister Sal in her highchair to notice. He refrained from reaching to scratch his back where he itched from the grass, a reaction he always got from new spring shoots. Once, when he and his best friend Mike rolled down Sotter's Hill in their underwear, his mum had to take him to the doctor for antibiotic cream. But this time he didn't scratch, and he didn't mind. All through dinner he recalled lying in the grass with Mary, how he'd taken his shirt off in the hot afternoon sun, how they'd found the softest spot at the edge of the trees, how he'd kept still as he possibly could and never run out of things to say while the breeze whispered across his shoulders, her neck and knees.

Close your eyes

Close your eyes, she said.

She took my hand in hers: warm, dry, sure. She led my fingers up her arm, around her elbow. *My body's a landscape*, she said.

She laid out a map of her life that night. That vein there: a long road down the back of her sun-freckled knee, slightly bumpy since the birth of her child. My fingers skipped up one smooth arm as she told of an easy childhood and laughed at the memories of tree forts and tea parties and the time she flew at seven, all alone, to visit her grandma in Tennessee. I navigated a gravel road up the other arm: teen years, cruel and rough, hard to describe but easy to imagine. A scar through the right eyebrow: daddy's mark. Butterfly kisses on my palm from long lashes she got from her mum. Further down the road, valleys gave way to mountains, and mountains proved worth climbing. I nestled into the pond scent of her belly, mossy and cool.

Close your eyes and you can see it all, she said.

Impossible weather

It's snowing in my heart, Jane says fancifully, but Terry doesn't hear her because he's deafened by his own smile as he turns and places a drink in her hand. He's already forgotten the argument from the night before. He's that kind of guy. He's sipping his own drink through a ridiculously long straw. It's one of those bluish drinks with a happy pink umbrella, one of those drinks that cost much too much. Jane's is similar but her straw is yellow. The drink and his smile should be enough to melt the snowflakes icing up her heart. She sips. It's one of those drinks that are much too sweet but with crushed ice like sparkly Christmas lights it cools her off under the tropical sun. She slides her sunglasses to the top of her head, a familiar gesture he adores. He reaches out and tucks a loose wisp of hair behind her left ear. A gentle touch. He's impossibly happy as he starts talking about the afternoon activities – tennis, then volleyball on the beach with Sarah and Jim, two unbearably likeable Americans that seem to live an eerily parallel life and whom Terry has adopted as his new best friends. Following tennis, there are his-and-her massages. Then dinner for two, or for four if Sarah and Jim show up. Terry has planned this weekend getaway for her birthday. Jane can't decide which part of the rest of this day she dreads most.

~~~
~~~

It's snowing in my heart, Jane says again just before dinner, but she says it mostly to the closet where her array of silk dresses hang. She can't decide which one to choose so she leaves them swaying breezily on their hangers and does everything else: hair, makeup, bracelets, watch, necklace (the new one), perfume. She reaches around the back to fasten her bra but knows this is one of those nights they'll fuck right after dinner so she slips into a thong then out again just as Terry pulls a dress from the closet, says, *This one*. It's the emerald one, the one he says matches her golden eyes. She steps into it and pulls it on slowly. She knows he's noticed the dropped thong in the centre of the room. She knows he'll think of it lying there in a lacy sigh all through dinner. He'll think on it from duck to sorbet. He will not be able to linger and talk to the unbearably likeable Americans but instead will reach for her thigh and guide her away from the table after she drinks the last warm drops of champagne. Back in their room he'll lift her soft emerald dress over her shoulders and leave it there as they fall onto the bed. Her arms will be caught up over her head, wrapped in green silk. As he slips into her she will wonder if he could peer all the way down through her golden eyes and see the weather in her heart. Then, with a thrust that is surely his love and a sigh that is surely her yielding, she wonders if the snowflakes could be melting, just a little.

~~~
~~~

It's snowing in my heart, Jane says over breakfast berries and cream. But Terry's not there. He's already down at the shore, wading out into the turquoise water. He comes back mid-morning, just as a squall rolls in from the sea and darkens the island. *Next holiday*, he says, leaning over to kiss her shoulder and dripping a little ocean into her hair. *I was thinking about the Tyrol. Skiing. Hiking. You know. Too much sun can be bad for your health.* She nods and looks out the window. The squall is coming in fast. She can see its shadow haunting the reef. A downpour will strike within minutes. *They never get the forecast right, do they,* he says, as he pulls her up to him. He smiles his impossible smile and she feels wet. She cannot resist his touch. She likes the sex. She likes him. They make love on the veranda as the rain pours down. She feels his warmth hovering like clouds. She sweats. She wants to tell him she loves him. She thinks she loves him. He rolls off her and starts planning their ski holiday. The rain stops as suddenly as it began.

X

I.
Do you remember, brother, when we were kids, how you laughed at my crush on Bill? How you mocked the letters I wrote when he went to boarding school, the *x* I added after my name?

II.
My crush lasted till he sent a photo: arms flung around a roommate's shoulders, huge Confederate flag on the wall. You said, *Don't hold it against him,* but I did.

III.
You're too political, you said, *with your Malcolm X posters and DC rallies.* I laugh at that now, 'cause who's fighting the fight? Who turned patriot overnight?

IV.
We sat on your porch, singing *The Fourth of July* with Exene and John. You lit a Camel. I grinned, recalling when I begged one off you and gagged and you said, *Smoking ain't pretty.*

-Do you have to go?
-No.
-But you're gonna go?
-Yeah.

V.
I sign every letter to you with an x.

VI.
I looked up your camp, marked it: x. I couldn't say the name, just wanted to see it on my globe, halfway round the world from here.

VII.
I wrote a desert story, called it *Homecoming*. It was no good so I cut it right out of my system, *ctrl-x*.

VIII.
Phone call from Mum. Merry fucking Xmas. The screams spilled over the linoleum and took my voice. I've not spoken since.

IX.
Your letter arrived today. It's in my pocket, unopened.
-Promise you'll write?
-Cross my heart, hope to die.
I stare at the letter, mouth dry with sand and sorrow.

X.
On your porch, a step you never fixed. Your letter burns my pocket. If I open it, your voice will drift into the still night. I marvel at your tiny neat print, the black *x* written after your name. I sit, smoke a cigarette alone.

Roll the die

THREE. Past present future. Which path, eh? Past is dead. Never mind Faulkner. Present: a maze. Future: Don't go there. Roll again, boy.

SIX. Count the days since you spoke. Draw a line in the sand. Stay still: stop where you are. Don't talk don't listen don't blink. Don't break don't breathe don't think. Throw the die once more and…

ONE. Easy. Stop. Broken. Repair? Listen. Sleep. Again.

FIVE. Can't sit still, not now. Slipping, sleeping, in and out. This moment, a fleeting free-for-all. A dream-state spinning roulette table. Black-red-black-red-black. Five words in a promise. *I will never leave you.* You thought *Never say never.* But you didn't say it.

FOUR. You blow for luck. Which works, it seems…

– 'cause this time you're down on the Wannsee, wading in the shallows, sister grinning goofy, Mum laying out the picnic. Dad's there untangling the rigging on your model sailboat. He'll make it work this time. He always makes it work. You are happy you are happy you are happy – again. The past is dead but it's a good dream still and –

Wake up, roll again. Dreams aren't really real. *This* is: game's ending. Hold on, hold it. Squeeze the die, squint. Roll it, believe it.

Two. Morning light. Sticky thoughts. And him.

Pocket him. Shoot him. Fuck him. Consume him.
Hum him. Sing him. Burn him. Love him.
Forget him. Forever him.

Wake up.

Wanderer

They met on a mountaintop in the Pyrenees. When she slipped and he steadied her, his hand on her elbow, she jerked herself away. *Got to keep moving.*

It was the truest thing she ever told him. He followed her around Europe for a year: floating on the Dead Sea so salty their afterward kisses stung; reviving their bodies in Iceland's massaging mud baths; climbing ancient hills in Greece that made them giddy with history.

By the time she started admitting they were a couple they'd been through three bedrolls. The other gear had held up well – their backpacks, and her tent, which had become their home.

"Come to New Zealand with me," he said, for the third time. This day he thought she might say yes.

"Maybe."

Three months later she flew to Kerikeri to meet him but she didn't stay long. *Got to keep moving.*

She trekked across the South Island and camped along the Abel Tasman trail. She made her way from the black sands of Muriwai to the soft beaches of the Bay of Islands.

It was when she was in the far north, at Cape Reinga, perched at the edge of a cliff off to the side of the crowded tour buses come to see the jumping off place for travelling souls, that she felt something move inside her. She didn't call him for two more weeks.

When he found her, she took his hand and led him down a hill to a small cove. Her hand felt small but sure, and her fingers laced gently in his. At the sandy beach, she pulled a canister from her backpack. He watched as she unwrapped a green scarf tied around it, unscrewed the lid, and tossed the contents out to sea. The breeze caught the grey dust and swirled some of it back on them; other bits plunked into the water at their feet.

They stood silent together for a long while, their heartbeats working in time to the waves breathing in and out along the shoreline. Some of the ashes stayed floating in the tide at their feet.

"There," she said. "It's done."

"You never said."

"I never could. But my children belong here." She placed his palm on her belly. "Both of them."

She was surprised when she realised she meant it. She was surprised that she imagined herself at home here, stacking firewood with him in winter, sailing a small boat out the Kerikeri River in summer.

She had carried the stillborn baby's remains, so small they hardly took any space in her pack, for three years. Now she could see four seasons in front of her, and they rolled by as if in natural order.

A fierce southerly blew that night through their tent at Taputopotu Bay. Tears finally came in the morning: at the ashes still streaking her jeans, at the Pacific which now rocked her first-born away, at the blood-orange sun already warming her forearms. She recalled what someone had told her: that the sun shines brighter here, that you must be careful not to get burned.

He found her swaying at the water's edge. He was sure she would drift away with the tide or float back north on the wind if he touched her.

Finally he spoke. "And now?"

She turned and said, "We begin."

Morning flash

A hush in the air. Frost glows and mist whispers. A silver sheen covers the cool earth: a hovering blanket on a slumbering world. I stand in a shadowstill meadow; before me stretches an Asian painting on canvas, a China doll landscape, delicate and glassy, almost without colour. It looks as if it might shatter if I move. That is how still it is. Then. A tiny snowdrop waving, a hint of green winking from the branch of that tall tree. The chickadee's *phoebe* and the titmouse's *peter peter* greeting the longer days. Light spreading across the world. Dew and sweat and life itself, a new-born calf shivering in the barn. Soon this meadow will crescendo in colour and erupt in a thunder of delightful spring noise. I will let loose and run.

Idea for a long documentary film

after Lydia Davis, with a nod to the German film Männer

Representatives of **X** are given **Y** for opening **Z**.

The film takes place in a paternoster lift.

(And necessarily includes tangential explorations of the history of the paternoster lift and the fight against its extinction.)

Directed by Werner Herzog.

The Fuddy-Duddy Editor Gets Real: Write Like You Write

You want to write like Lydia Davis? You think that'll get you published?

She's good at what she does. Everyone wants to write like LD. But you can't and you won't.

Write a story of apples or watermelon, write about geography; converse with history, talk to your dead brother; write loss, write a list. Try everything. See where you go.

Don't listen to anyone who tells you to write like someone else. Write like you write.

The Fuddy-Duddy
Editor Intrudes

The Fuddy-Duddy Editor Started Out As A Fuddy-Duddy Writer

For WB, founder and chair of WUC,BWUTC (We Use Colons, But We Use Them Correctly), editor and writer of fictions and poetry increasingly sprawling in size and shape, passionate and indecisive about punctuation

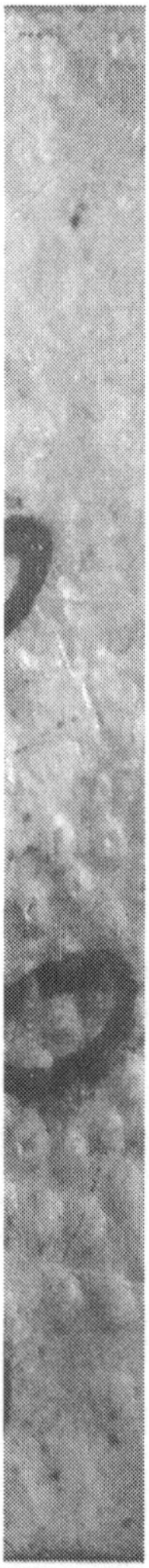

The Fuddy-Duddy Editor was once upon a time a writer. She shot to fame all right. But she did not rest on her laurels. She enjoyed the festival that was all about her, but she moved on. She lived fully in the moment, all the more so when the moment was all about her. She granted interviews, collected fanmail, never said no to a television appearance – better if it was not a panel; she was enough to fill a panel. She took to heart her fans' comments, and sometimes even replied.

When one fan sent her a cassette with The Meters' 'My Name Up in Lights', she shut herself in with her set of Broadway tunes,

landed on 'When I Get My Name in Lights' and sang it all day. The fan's heart was in the right place, but The Meters were too hip for the Fuddy-Duddy Writer, even if her nimble knees got to kicking it up that morning (before she recovered her senses) and even if she strutted outrageously, imagining herself way up that flagpole (way before she recovered her senses).

The Fuddy-Duddy Writer Reflects On Her Fan(s)

The Fuddy-Duddy Writer appreciates her fan, so devoted to her cause. He sends poems daily. This one arrived this morning:

Kids!
I don't know what's wrong with these kids today!
Kids!
Who can understand anything they text or say?
Kids!
Noisy, crazy, dirty, lazy punctuators!
While we're on the subject:
Kids!
You can text and twitter till your face is blue!
Kids!
But they still keypad what they want to do!
Why can't they be like we were,
Perfect punctualists in every way?
What's the matter with kids today?
Kids!

It is this fan who pushes her from a Fuddy-Duddy Writer to a Fuddy-Duddy Editor (and now Sometimes Writer). She has kids of her own, after all. She *likes* kids. She is learning to fud and dud her way a little less forcefully these days.

And really, the Fuddy-Duddy Writer has only one fan.

The Fuddy-Duddy Writer Looks For Her Story

Dear Story,

Where are you? I've been looking for nearly five days now. Perhaps you are under the chair, with the sticky breakfast crumbs. Or maybe you are outside, breathing in morning dew or perching on the washing line between those two red socks, or squeezing creek mud between your toes as you huddle with the mallards. You could be in the soup I made yesterday, bubbling in the broth with the carrots and peas. Or you could be resting on my downy pillow, nestled in the warm soft white where I lay my head.

I saw you last night in the sideways glance of my lover. I heard you this morning in my child's singsong voice.

You are a space-walker and a time-traveller, for, even as you jump across continents and oceans, and though you live very much in the present, you sometimes come to me from an obscured

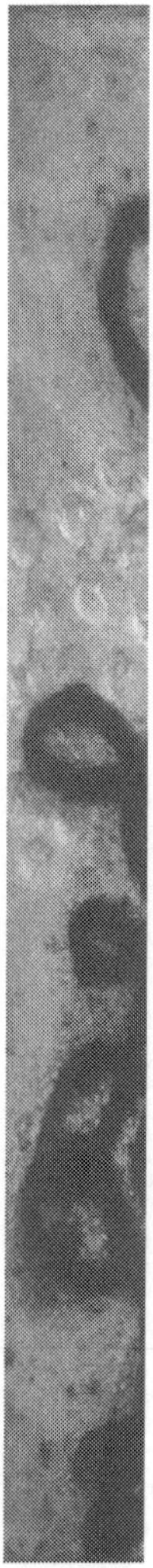

corner of the past, and you often feel
like the future, full of promise.

I will wait patiently, will not rush you.
You'll come. With a whisper or a shout, a
tickle or a punch.

Sometimes you are the thing itself.
Sometimes you hide

in the spaces between.

Sometimes you are the nothing of every day.

The Fuddy-Duddy Writer Explores Her Childhood: Dodge Ball

This is a story about a skinny girl named Penny. We climbed the monkey bars after school because my dad was usually late to pick me up and her parents arrived even later than my dad. So even if we didn't exactly intend to be friends, we were – *after* school, at least, since *during* school she was the kind who didn't dodge the red ball, and I was the kind who threw it hard because I could. I reckon I wasn't the nicest kid, but Penny saw past that simple kind of meanness. I didn't realise we were friends until one week she didn't turn up at school and I didn't talk to or play with anyone or even try hard in gym class. When she showed up again on the following Monday, I asked her name. And we became friends – probably even *BFF*s except this was before the age of *txt*ing everything to death and I already had a keen sense that *forever* was bullshit. When we had an outbreak of lice at school Penny took

me to her house and we shaved our heads with an electric razor. My teacher called my dad for a conference but he wasn't a conference kind of dad so he never showed. We kept our hair short all through that spring. By the following September, Penny had moved away and my hair had grown out.

The Fuddy-Duddy Writer Explores Her Childhood: Swimming Pool

When I was around seven, Pop had the idea to sell bottled water. Everyone laughed at him, said he was bonkers.

Which was true, mostly. He usually had one idea on the go, another in his back pocket. We were always *up-and-coming*. He started a swimming pool company once: we'd make it rich that way. We even built one, must have been the summer of '74 or '75. There are pictures of my oldest brother surveying the back yard, barely tall enough to peek through the lenses balanced on the orange tripod, and my other brother and me in the hopper, towelling aggregate smooth. Blonde kids up to their elbows in grey.

When the water trucks came, we had not yet put the braces in behind the walls so they began to push out with the weight of the water. The bolts groaned as the sides nearly pulled apart. I didn't know

something so liquidy smooth could be so heavy. "Quick, grab what you can!" We created our own landfill behind the walls, collected everything from our garage that we could find that was destined for the dump: old strollers, tents, games, trikes. So many items got buried that day.

Pop never did launch his water company. I reckon he should have. He's long gone, and we moved away. But I loved that pool, skinny-dipped my way through my teen years with my best friend Deb.

The Fuddy-Duddy Editor Goes To Berlin: And Then They Danced

Once upon a time there was a man who loved trains. He rode a train to work. He vacationed in old-timey steam engines, took his family on countryside train-rides. He dreamed about trains that lit up all corners of his city, that didn't speed through dark spaces where no one got out. He built a model railroad in his basement, with trees and mountains and people and villages and trains that went wherever they wanted to.

Once upon a time a girl met the man who loved trains. He took her to his basement and showed her his little city. He walked her out back, along the train tracks as far as they went, which was not very far at all, because overgrown weeds greened over rusty red, and just beyond was a wall that could not be climbed. The man told her of a past she knew from books: airstrikes and airlifts, hunger and hope. His life was in those tracks.

Once upon a time the man and the girl danced together, smashed concrete with hammers, thumbed their noses at ol' Erich and laughed at outdated regimes. Trains rumbled behind his house again.

Once upon a time, the man who loved trains was dying. The girl recalled the tiny free world, and the bigger walled world. She remembered *Tanzen* and *Klopfen*, the feel of history's concrete weight in her hands. She remembered the way the old man and his city lived a life that always got better.

The Fuddy-Duddy Editor Plays Scrabble

She looked at the board in front of her, the words criss-crossing in neat rows, the red triple-word square waiting for the letters that would win the game. It had come down to this, the score so close that the last play would clinch it.

She turned over her newly selected letter, the smooth surface in her palm.

A winning combination?

She organised the letters in front of her, concealed behind their letter-wall. She placed the *r* in its place.

Just right: *r-u-i-n*.

Months' worth of anger flooded in – violent words and a recently thrown shoe that had left a dent in the door.

"Your turn," she said.

He glanced up, a serious piercing look.

k: his first letter down, red triple.

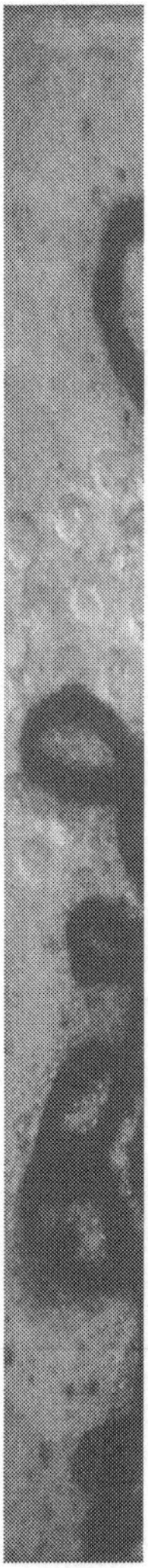

Then came the rest in rapid succession.

"That's not a word," she blurted. He was always a rule-breaker.
"I don't care."

The letters went flying as he reached across the table and pulled her to meet him half-way.
His *k-i-s-s-m-e* ending the game,
her *r-u-i-n* falling from its perch.

The Fuddy-Duddy Writer Is Thinking Of Breaking Up With Her Fan

The Fuddy-Duddy Writer is committed to her cause, but her fan wrote the following to her in an early morning email:

> *You actually may be the one person who can make your writer's life of abandon… as boring and mundane as in suburbia.*

She knows he struggles, this fan, with his own desire to see his name up in lights, and so she ignores his attempt at wit. The Fuddy-Duddy Writer does not do wit.

The Fuddy-Duddy Writer is thinking of breaking up with her fan.

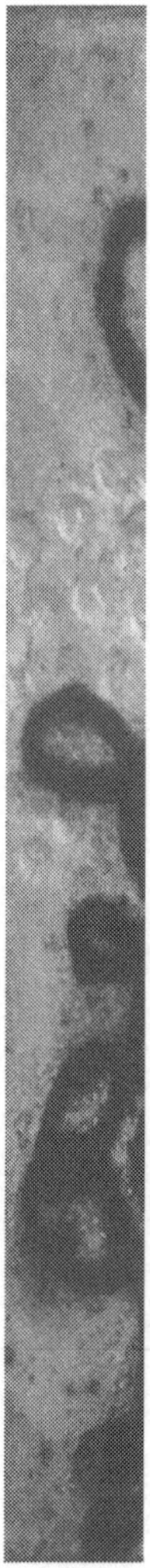

The Fuddy-Duddy Editor Dreams An Impossible Dream: Block Party

Voices call me out of sleep
groggy, curious, I creep
towards the kitchen,
   where the drinks are mixin'

This ain't my scene,
but I think I'll stay
– they're singing off-key
   won't you come out to play

You, Cheshire-grin, know-it-all:
   d'you like the party so far?
and you, boy in the spelling bee:
   how'd'you get from A to Z?
Butcher, baker, candlestickmaker:
   take your rhymes off my page!
(sigh)

I spy shitgreen Staasi-shirts marching by
– but wait, what's that? why are they drinking
with Wolf and Biermann?
What're they thinking?

That ain't right. They're not fighting the fight.
Everything's topsy turvy tonight:

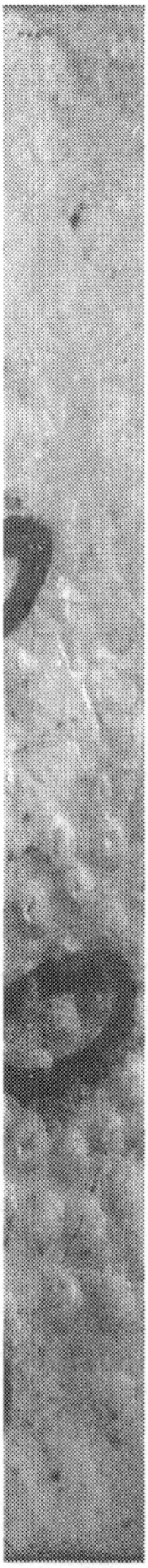

Hagen's singing cabaret, Liza's communing
with Krishna and Johnny's rotting
in the corner with scurvy.
Tamara sings 'Bye bye my love' and
we dance real slow,
build walls, turn west.

This Wall's my Wall – gotta mount it
go under over maybe round it
build it, climb it, Christo-bind it
find a way to nevermind it.

My catch-22: I want to keep all of you
here in my story, but I've got to
show some the door
there's a major cast,
a major twist,
with a major ending,
a major fist
fight in the toilet.

I can't sustain this frantic pace.
Got to trim, edit, cut, paste,
shut some of you up lest
you go and spoil it
(And who let in that
orangutan? he jumped
stories, he ain't part
of this plan!)

Gotta sleep, pull up the
cover
Let me know when the
party's
over

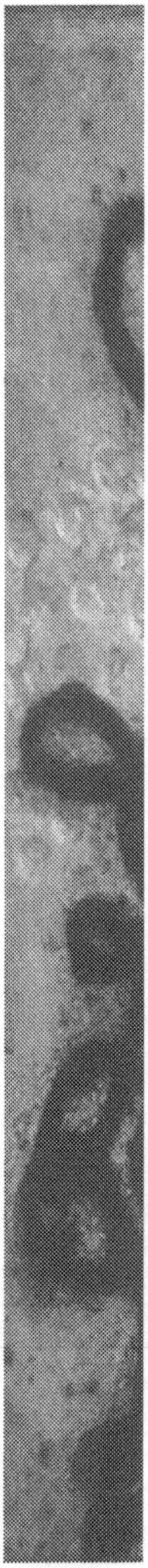

The Fuddy-Duddy Editor Reflects On The Importance Of Oral Hygiene: You Say Arugula, I Say Lettuce

I was surprised when Carrie called. We hadn't seen each other in years. We'd been high-school friends, the kind you don't expect to see again after you've been pomp-and-circumstanced down the school stadium steps and the last D-Major chord has drifted out on the breeze. But I'd just had my first baby and she'd had her second, so she called for a *mommy's* lunch.

At the upscale yuppy café ("my *fave*," she gushed), I ordered a baked stuffed potato (the closest thing to real food on offer) while she drank protein-vitamin-water and pushed sprigs of delicately arranged arugula around her plate.

We caught up: the husband/house/job/ childbirth list. She swooned about her offspring, who were home with the *au pair*, while mine nursed noisily in my lap.

I sought peace in my potato while she carried on about her dullard husband and McMansion. And her stupid onroad/ offroad jogging stroller – *the Landrover of strollers*. "I prefer my 1970 Pontiac Firebird," I offered, "which has seen my sister through five kids. It's named Blue Betty." Carrie grimaced. My wee angel farted marvellously.

When she said she could not stay for dessert, I masked my elation as she air-kissed my cheeks goodbye. She sashayed out of the café just as my chocolate mint parfait arrived. I watched her go, musing on the contrast between her perfectly heart-shaped jogger's ass and the green sprigs of lettuce stuck between her shiny white teeth.

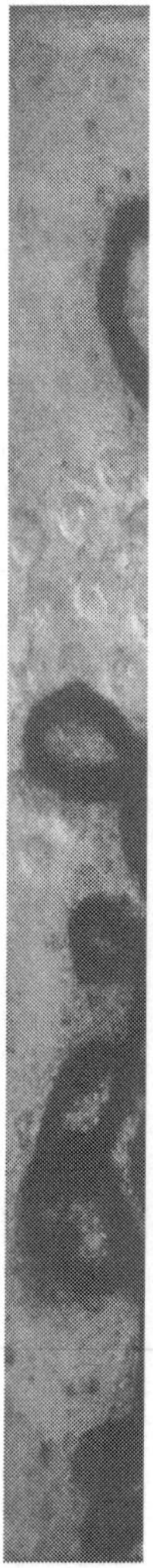

The Fuddy-Duddy Editor Breaks Out of Her Comfort Zone: French Kiss

The date began badly. First, she turned up her nose at my suggestion of sushi: "*Ew!* I want *real* food!" So we found ourselves at a picnic table eating hamburgers and fries, hers dipped in a large dollop of mayo.

Back in the car, she switched the radio from Waits to Madonna. Crossed my mind I should kick her out.

I suggested wine at my place (she was French, after all), but she said, "No, that's *boring*," and next thing I know we're down by the lake drinking Jaegermeister. Haven't drunk that stuff since uni. I managed not to puke this time, even when she said, "I'm going to fuck you now, *oui*?" I was powerless in her hands, her mouth. She scared the hell out of me, from her rock-hard nipples to her abundant thighs to her curious tongue. I envisioned news flashes next day: *Culture Clash: Carnivorous Frenchie Fucks Shy Biology Teacher Dead*. She was all energy, grinning and grinding, sound and sexual fury. I ached for days, especially where my knee wedged into the dashboard. How she fit all those ways I never did figure.

I kept her number for a long time. "Call me," she said as she slipped the paper into my jeans pocket. Not a question, more a demand. I wanted to, I really did.

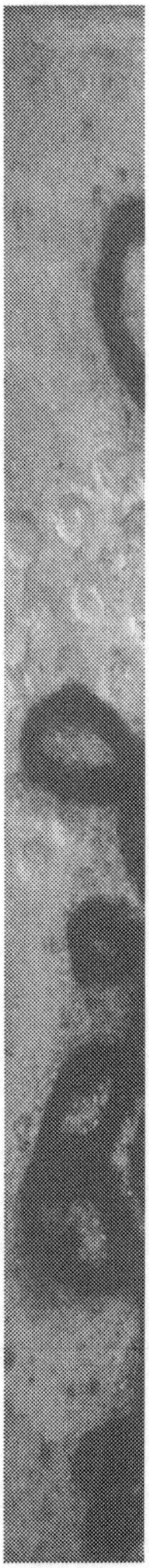

The Fuddy-Duddy Editor Knows Her Limits

The Fuddy-Duddy Editor admits to never really taking to Lydia Davis' short short fiction.

(But she likes her novel. And she named her cat Lydia.)

(Go figure.)

The Fuddy-Duddy Editor In The New Year

She slept in dreams of gold. Everything
exploding
beautiful
wondrous

the opposite of frightening.

They left her feeling calm and light,
these dreams.

House-job-commute: kapow!
Broke-down car: kapow!
Cheaters and liars: kapow!

She lined up those things and said (or
did not say because it was a dream after
all): *Off with your head!* And their heads
fell right off. Just like that.

It happened, too, with the flick of a wand (she had a wand, somewhere, and she might have even yelled *Abracadabra!*), or maybe just a withering glance (that worked too).

Simultaneously all those things exploded,
evaporated,
dissipated into thin air.

Even the yappy dog from next door: one raised eyebrow did him in.

A year's worth of jammed up stuff was simply
gone.

The air was clean and she could breathe.
In her dreams.

She woke to the lingering giddy golden light.

She opened her eyes: the water-stained ceiling.

She opened her ears: the whir of the fan.

She freed her arms from the dull grey sheets hanging heavy on her body.

She rolled over to the colourless lump in the bed beside her, snoring and oblivious.

She leaned across to the bedside table, whiffed something ripe, fermentation: a thing past its due date.

She rose from the bed, looked back over her shoulder, whispered: *kapow!*

She took nothing with her.

She stepped into a wide, open space.

The Fuddy-Duddy Editor Is Working On Her Memoir

She is middle-aged by now. She is less Fuddy-Duddy and more … well, she nurtures her yoghurt cultures and does yoga. Her kids are glad she dumped her fan. Her memoir is called: *Life and Love with a Clean Colon.*

The Fuddy-Duddy Editor Reflects On Love

Running, tripping, falling backwards
Making deals with God or Devil
whichever is better

Radio's on, Bush is burning. Turn up
your devil grin your thunder heart, or God
whichever is better

– love is loud

Listen
breathe out, in
and soon in tune

a song

on the other side

in a dream
in a dream
in a dream

Time to rest

One grey day the earth decided to sleep. The mighty mountains shrugged their rounded shoulders and sighed a great necessary sigh. The wide seas sucked their liquid breath in and out in deep soothing swells. The earth turned inward. Oil stopped flowing. The flat plains coughed a dry cough and the mantis-like machines creaked to a halt. The ocean floor sneezed a satisfying sneeze and swallowed the drilling platforms whole. People who lived on the planet scurried around noisily looking for shelter, and those who could took flight to new frontiers. Some – the quiet ones – stayed behind, and made peace with the sleeping mother.

Soon, all activity ceased and the only thing audible was the sound of sleep in a world that emerged ecstatic with fragrance and colour. Tiare and jasmine shouted happy stories across continents, magnolias made mad love as their roots stretched deep into the wet fertile soil, while sequoia and kauri reached with their arms towards heaven.

And the mighty mountains sighed, and the wide seas heaved.

And the earth dreamed blue-green dreams.

Elephant

They say we can't jump, and they're probably right,
but I've never tried, truth be told.

They say they're in charge. They say. They say they
believe in conservation, in protection.

They say they want to save the oceans-beaches-trees-
lakes-you-name-it. Us. They say.

They make Animal fucking Planet but I never watch it.
I'm here with too much sun and sky and the scorching
earth and not enough water for my baby.

They say they love animals, they got details to prove it.
They collect lists.
    Bulls are colourblind.
    Butterflies were flutterbies.
    Polar bears are lefties, snails like to sleep.

Do the details matter? Do they know my grief?
It's not in their fact list, but it is real.

Listen:

I am a whale of a being, and I barely exist.
I have been here for millennia.
My mind stretches
across space and time
and knows the softest part of skin,
the taste of my mother,
the sound of my brother,
the smell of life, the touch
of memory.

Urine is essence.

I piss gallons on what they say.

Giraffe types a letter

One day Giraffe got herself a typewriter and sat down with her long fingers (she got a set of those, too, because how else could a giraffe type) and wrote a letter to the people up the road, the ones who work in offices with food carts outside their buildings, who spend days pushing around ideas, sometimes lobbing them high into the air, then watching them float back to earth in their little badminton birdie ways, these ideas never meant to get much lift and always falling back to earth. When she finished she read the letter aloud and, finding it wholly unsatisfying, ripped it out of the machine, like you see in the old movies *rrrrrrriiiiiiiipppppp!,* and tore it up. The paper made a sighing sound, and confettied away in the East African wind. She sat back down at her typewriter (slowly slowly – because that's the only way a giraffe can sit down) and began again. But that one wasn't right either, so Giraffe wrote a third letter, and a fourth, and a fifth, until she pulled the last from the typewriter with a pleasing *rrrriiiiiiipppp!* She looked for typos because giraffes are careful about such things. She stood, sniffed; the ancient earth smelled good, with its red-soil rain-round-the-bend scent.

Giraffe stretched to her full four metres and showed Daughter her letter. Daughter read it thoughtfully because she's born-that-way-smart and blinked once, then twice, her lush lashes chasing the flies from her eyes. Then she shrugged, moving off to the nearest acacia and said, over her shoulder, Come, Ma, this tall one here, its scent is perfect.

Aquinas, acid and me

I am sloth, sluggish on my mossy tree. There is a limb reaching towards me, a bridge to another tree if only I can move. But it's too far and it's not my nature to try. I didn't get this nickname for nothing.

It is quiet here. I am floating up. There is no stronghold, not a single holdfast. Now, when I am about to float away, I hear a faint song, not recognisable, a soft surprise as it plays backwards. I settle onto my branch and watch the world unwind. A flutterby turns back into chrysalis: the anti-pupate, no cocoon, no safety. I look back and see what lies ahead. I look ahead and see you behind me. Not where I left you.

What is your name? I say.

Saniuqa.

Is that Spanish?

No. You are not at home. And listen: sloth is not a sin, it's passion.

I am passion, I say. I will bite the apple, but then I am stained red. I am muscle fibre under a microscope and you are looking hard at me, with your cheap Cory Hart sunglasses.

Shhh, you say, *Listen*. You take out a vinyl LP, play it backwards. It scratches just the same. I like the sound.

Eosin is an anagram of noise, you say.

I take the LP and play it all the way home as it unwraps, unwinds and undoes everything I know.

Longing

"Come on down," she said, and he did. Hopped right on a plane after a two-month romance that began online. The electricity pulled him right round the globe, from the safety of the frozen north to the turquoise waters of the South Pacific.

It was good, too. They surfed on virgin beaches by day and gazed at phosphorescent dolphins by night. He was lulled to sleep by the sound of midnight waves and her deep sea voice. She was soothed by his big man laugh and thrilled by his big city stories, the ones with Lenny, Scanio, and Bruce.

But soon the red curry sun and coconut cream love wasn't enough. He found himself longing for home.

"You could come with me," he said. "Skate down my hill with a view of Manhattan, see the world from the Staten Island ferry, eat lemon ices."

She puckered her lips, thought *How could you not love a place called Bliss Park?*

"Yes, I think I could," she said.

He told more of his street where polka and soul sang on the same summer breeze, where a foghorn came through his early morning window – the same foghorn Walt Whitman heard when he was writing. He described all that he longed to share with her.

She wrapped her blue shawl tight around her shoulders, leaned into him. She loved these stories of Whitman and polkas and Italian ice. But they belonged to this Brooklyn boy, and she belonged here.

Juggler

I used to be a juggler. Got pretty good, too. Started out small, used three beanies my flatmate Stefan gave me. Stefan was a lively juggler, could use anything at hand. I once watched him grab a salt shaker, a wine glass, and a roll of toilet paper and toss them in the air. I held my breath, expected them to come crashing down on the floor, but he kept them suspended for five minutes. All while belting out Nina Hagen.

So I started juggling with Stefan every Sunday in the Stadtpark. I was terrible at first. *Man, you gotta breathe,* he'd laugh. Breathing helped. I could even ride a unicycle. We started busking and we breathed and balanced our way all over Germany. Made some money, got another partner in our act. Beate could swallow swords. But she left us eventually for a poet named Peter in Paris, and after that the chemistry was gone. Stefan went back to Hamburg, I flew home to Pennsylvania. Found myself in a cubicle wearing polyester shirts and simultaneously drinking sherry from a flask I kept hidden in my bottom drawer while suffocating.

Now I'm back in Hamburg, wondering what happened to Stefan after all this time. I go to the Stadtpark on Sundays and juggle. I'm not so good anymore but there's a girl with red shoes who keeps her distance but always watches. I'm going to talk to her one of these days.

How to make lolo

Fun comes in large doses round here, babes swinging in tyres, boys climbing wrecked hulls, girls excavating hermit crabs. Your Carolina towhead's right at home among these island kids. You've been here one month now but it may as well be three or four. Time has stopped. Everything is different. He is gone, swallowed silently by the swirling Pacific. Not a trace of his life was found. Not a single piece of clothing, not a molecule – though you suppose his atoms are currently reforming from solid to liquid to gas. Absorbed, universal.

Your daughter glances up from the water's edge, flips her hand like a small fish, back and forth, back and forth. Wet, slippery, shiny. Pretty against the bright Fijian sky. Her baby teeth flash, too. Each year, she will look more like him. You can see her cowlick from here, errant hair standing at attention from her small head. Like his. You wave back though your arm feels heavy. The other kids all wave now: a game. Swish, swish go their brown hands, flashing against the backdrop of sea and sky.

Why did you stay? Why aren't you back home with family, school, alarm clocks? With paved roads leading the way to and fro, lines marking a clear direction and traffic lights blinking *Stop, Go*?

You sit on the low porch, grating coconut with Kalesi, knees gripping the large bowl. You follow her expert strokes, her strong arms, wanting to do it just right. As if there is order in these small tasks. Order and the promise of something sweet.

She pours water into the bowlful of fluffy white clouds, dives in with both hands and pulls her fingers up through the murky liquid. Soft coconut cream runs in rivers to your elbows and you sob, punching at memory, fists on thighs. Kalesi brushes away fury and noise, smoothes away your hair with rough knuckles.

Behind the house, the men tend the fire and pound kava. Soon they will unwrap the banana leaves and bring the food to the porch. Chicken, cassava, taro leaves. Sometimes they throw in Maggi instant noodles. Bury the food and cook it slowly; everything tastes good that way. The small fish boil on the gas burner. They will be eaten, too, down to every small bone. The kids will fight over the succulent eyeballs.

Later you climb into bed with your child, breathe in her sweet salt skin, spy a speck in her white-blonde hair, then another. You pinch lice between finger and thumb. You will scrub her scalp in the morning.

Black and white and grey

In the gloaming she sees his tall shape across the street, hunched shoulders under a black coat slumped to worry. She steps off the kerb and hurries to him. She wants to ask him *how was your meeting, did you get the red wine for dinner, do you remember that the Lamberts are coming*, but it's cold and the wind hurts her teeth so she lifts her head slightly to the left instead and as she slips her palm into his she feels him grip her small hand and squeeze tight.

In the gloaming he sees her silhouette crossing the street, small neat steps with white socks peeking from under tailored trousers. He wants to tell her *they read my father's will today, my brother says my sister won't come, I forgot to get the red wine for dinner*, but he feels a chill on his spine and in the moment that she tilts her head towards him he knows he doesn't love her but he squeezes her hand anyway and notices that her grey felt cap looks just right.

Snapper

A cold platinum day. The waves roll in like timpani. Surfers dot the water like seals, eager for the rollick and rush of the next big one. Francie and Jack ride the same wave in. He follows her up the beach, wants to kiss her shivering lip first time he sees it. She slips her wetsuit off her shoulders and rolls it down her torso. She knows he is watching. She mounts her board on top of her car, turns and says *Let's build a fire.* They sit close but do not touch, sip whisky from his flask. She's in flames by the time he says *Let's eat.*

~~~

Snapper for tea. Jack fillets it expertly, the blade slipping under the flesh, his fingers knowing exactly how to move over the meat. Francie eyes his snapper hands, feels heat crawl up her neck and down her thighs. She sits at the table, waits. They share a beer, pushing it between them, and slide snapper into each other's mouths, fingertips barely touching lips. They don't make it all the way to bed. Naked in front of the fire that warms them against the cool late-summer air, she moves in silence, fingers tugging salty hair, straining to the chirruping of grasshoppers. She likes the sound of friction.

~~~

Hot copper sun. The black sands of Muriwai melt in the unexpected heat wave. A new flame is fuelled by alcohol, noise: timpani made by temper. Jack's mood has turned hot with the wind, dark as the sands. They have argued for days – about what, they can't say. Francie takes her board and paddles alone into the surf, kids' tinny voices in the distance. She returns at sunset to find him waiting, three empties glinting in the sand. Her lips purse. He glares. She knows what she wants. *Snapper*.

Earl Grey

It happened in the library. She sat at a table cluttered with poetry books. I came in from the rain, took the only empty chair.

Tea? she asked. Like tea belonged there. Like *I* belonged there, my soggy newspaper flopped between Frost and Frame.

"You study poetry?"

"The Fs this week," she said, pouring a cup for me. Cloves wafted up. We talked an hour. After she left, I could only recall the sound of her white plastic raincoat crinkling at her elbows as she collected her things.

Next week, Ginsburg and Goethe. I muttered something feeble about Faust; she suppressed a sly smile. I slurped peppermint, recalled a limerick but fuckit the girl from Nantucket did not belong here.

We sat together several more times. Hughes (citrus), then Ibsen and Joyce and Keats (black and green and oolong).

Then one day, she was there with no poets. "Come on," she said. I panted up four flights behind her swishy raincoat, entered her neat apartment speechless and sweaty.

"No more tea," she said, rounding on me with surprising fierceness. "Except in the morning: Earl Grey for breakfast." She swigged from a whisky bottle then opened her mouth, pulled me in.

The next morning, she told me her name.

Up the creek

Up the Henderson Creek you may find an orchard of apples and plums. They are ripe and ready to pick, and there are storerooms for their sweetening.

Up the creek you may find a brick archway, carefully constructed of Auckland bricks as the entrance to the storerooms. You will see how this arch presides over a swimming hole, where echoes of Henderson youth still ring out.

Up the creek you may venture into the storeroom where apples once filled the space in sacks. You may find another room, dry and cool, and here you may elect to sit down and read a volume of the Encyclopaedia Britannica, too.

And also up the creek you may find the *Awatea*, sitting old and tired in the mud – a ship designed for glorious sailing and then secreted away.

You may ask this ship why she sits and waits. She will tell you she is patient, and does not mind the wait. She knows that her rig was built strong and her cabin top sturdy. She knows her knees and ribs hold on with time. She awaits the man who will come and first free her, and then another, and another – all of whom will strip her rusting rigging and rebuild her rotten cabin top and tear off the copper sheathing on her hull to restore the still strong kauri underneath. She fared well up the creek. She has never complained.

Sign language

They come to watch us. Sometimes they sit for days. They scratch with their scratchy little hands, they nod with their noddy little heads. They whisper, as if we won't notice them.

We see them. We see it all.

But we go about our business and act as if they're not there. Sometimes a younger one of us will get curious and stop, even go up close, smile. Sometimes an older one will walk in circles in front of them, dragging her sad knuckles on the ground, pacing, pausing, pacing some more.

They jot. They whisper.

Sometimes they take us away and inject us, massage us, pull and poke us. We leave better than we arrived so we don't say anything and return to the forest (our *habitat*) mended, better than before. And that's nice really. Nice to feel mended.

But still, I get annoyed. Sometimes, I curl my cutesoft palm into a ball and then unfold the middle finger (I slow it down for effect: *one, two, three…*) and then I unroll it at the labcoat, but before I know it I'm flipping the bird at all of you, at you in your university tower and you in your fuck-the-EU attitude and you with your walls and you with your Neonazis and you with your unsavable refugees and you with your unjailable poachers and you with your fingers on the button and you with your neon-coloured White House. At you, coming here to mend us.

At you, jotting. At you, whispering.

Hippo talks shit

They got nothin' on us, those monkeys, them with their silly poo – so tiny, so hard, not nearly smelly enough.

We got some serious shit. Just watch it fly.

Them little guys with their skinny arms. Ha! Look at my appendage: 14 inches of muscle, and a neat little tuft of hair at the end.

I can really swish.

It's so effortless, my stink. And I'm a vegetarian.

Well, sorta. I like the occasional mammal who gets in my way, comes yapping about all the beauty, the vastness, the magical sense of Africa, *blahblahblah.*

You want a real show? Come to the watering hole, some three hundred of us, babies crawling over mamas and sisters and brothers and who knows who, swimming and bottomwalking, grandfathers farting worse than yours ever did when he couldn't stop his bowels and everyone felt so apologetic about the whole thing.

We don't know apologetics.

We let it rip. Wet, smelly, beyond smelly –
in the words of the small girl (Which small girl, you ask? Every small girl…):
ewwwwwwwww.

And just look in my gape: that 150-degree angle! those incisors! It's rumoured I'm the most dangerous animal in the world.

So go on, write up those chimps over at the lake, jot in your fancy notebooks, hold your pencils just so with your own little chimpy hands. Consider this: my closest relation is the *whale*.

We talk underwater.

Nothing happens at sea

"Nothing happens at sea," he had told her, and for the most part he was right. Mile after mile is the same: the blue sea-skyscape he'd always known, the slow undulation of ocean swell, the maddening froth and staccato rhythm of storms, the constant hum of wind over canvas. An occasional pod of dolphins, an occasional albatross. An occasional moment of terror with an unfamiliar noise. An occasional evening symphony in the cockpit – sometimes Brahms, sometimes Zappa.

On this passage, there's Christmas pudding, too. Every day, because she gave it to him as a parting gift. She is in the pudding. She is everywhere.

He had laughed when she gave him the pudding, forty tins in all – one for every estimated day in the Southern Ocean – for the rich bricks will last much longer than his passage from Auckland to Punta Arenas. "So you won't forget me," she had said, patting the boxes gently.

"I will not forget you," he'd said.

"But will you come back?"

~~~
~~~

He sails east, looks over his shoulder with every sunset. He had not answered, for as sure as she is from there, he is from nowhere.

He hears her voice on the wind.

Paint

When we were kids, we cut out shapes   just
the right size for our small hands
we glued them down, some neat, some not
the teacher scolded, sometimes
    – *Draw inside the lines,*
    make your letters slant

We painted glue on our fingers, let it harden, bent
it off in long sticky strands, smooth, translucent

Once, you peeled a piece away and it looked
ghosty-grey   like a ship

We said then we'd sail across oceans – me
as star navigator and you with clouds   in your eyes

We said we'd build a boat and in our dreams
                                                              we believed it

We
said
our boat
would sail any
sea, with any wind,
and we cut out triangle
shapes, pasted them on the
grey classroom wall where they
floated all
year long

We dreamed of sailing oceans for months
and then the bell rang
and you moved
away

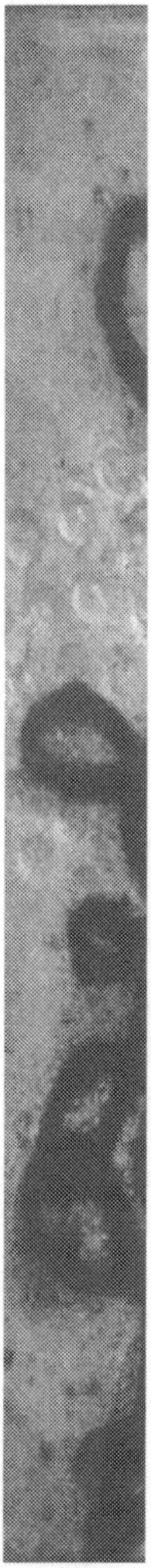

The Fuddy-Duddy Editor Nods In Agreement

Echoes of the sea – and John Barth: On with the story!

The long way

for Sian Williams

And then she stroked her last stroke and kicked her last kick. And Gemma found herself on an unfamiliar beach. Washed up. But alive. She tasted salt, heard the snuffle of a dog. And she smelled sun-sea-air: life itself. She crawled under a palm tree and slept for days, maybe years.

In a dream.

She dove deep into sleep, met Tangaroa. Asked for pocket change for the bus but he laughed, scolded her for wearing fins instead of growing them herself. She swam on smoothly, did not say *Goodbye* or *Nice to meet you.*

In a dream in a dream.

Gemma swam into a kelp forest, pulled herself down. When she got to the holdfasts, she kept going, deeper. It smelled damp and rotten all around her, but she liked it here, down under the root of things. She met root dwellers, small antlike creatures with lights in their windows, but she forgot to ask them for change, forgot the bus. Anyway, how could ants have change in their tiny pockets? But one told her to keep going. Gave her a surfboard and said his name was Bernard. *Moitessier*? – the first thing she'd said in days, maybe years. But he'd already vanished into the kelp forest.

In a dream in a dream in a dream.

So she took the long way. And years later Gemma landed, this time with a surfboard, here. A beach. A palm. A sleep. Frangipani floated on the air. She stroked the dog, named him Bernard.

New world

The baby was conceived on the day the earth slipped closer to the sun. Maré was not quite sure which came first: the flash of heat, the powerful orgasm, or the sun and moon suddenly a few millimetres closer within reach. Perhaps they happened concurrently, perhaps it was pure chance. She would never know, of course, but she felt in the ensuing weeks slightly guilty, as if she might have caused the slip with that one uncontrolled moment of lust and love. She had felt the world shift as she cried out repeatedly, not the hollow 'Oh God!' that accompanied earlier orgasms, real and imagined, but something more primal, more heartfelt, more natural. Something that came simultaneously from within her abdomen and from a source greater than any one individual.

Never mind the causes. The flash of love was real, the life within her was real, and the main thing now was to climb.

She set out and never stopped, searching for higher ground as the snow and ice melted off the tops of mountains and dripped at first slowly then in greater cascades and finally in waterfalls, down into every valley and rock crevice. Deserts filled, and people built platforms from which to save their electronics, for though the sun's closer proximity heated the earth almost overnight, it was the rising water they feared most. Maré did not mind; something guided her to the highest mountain and she climbed each week.

The father of the child gave up by Week 15. He gave it a shot, at least, but she didn't expect him to stay with her, or to understand her calm in the face of perceived calamity. She carried with her a certainty that grew stronger each day, and the marvellous memory of the Big Bang that started it all, and so they parted friends and she sent him back down the mountain to join the panicking crowds below, where he belonged.

And so she carried on alone, through week 16, 17, 18, 19... And the earth heated and filled, and her belly heated and filled. Newspapers and radios and televisions far below lamented the good old days of the Great Flood, wished for a mere 40 days and 40 nights, but Maré knew in her heart that 40 weeks was her reality, and all that mattered. Her belly grew with each week and she climbed higher and felt lighter. The thinning air did not press on her lungs; she felt full in all ways, elevated and elated. By Week 35 she knew she was close to the top. An energy lifted her and guided her, and she climbed, her belly swelling and leading her forward, each step lighter than the previous.

In the 40th week Maré breathed her last breath, just as the baby was born. There was no panic, no pain. Her contractions began on a Wednesday morning, and she found a flat rock and lay down, welcoming the end of her journey and the blessing that was this new life. She was grateful that she was here, alone, with the world of blue all around – blue sky above, and blue earth climbing up to meet her here at the highest peak. She wondered briefly what happened to the people below, how high they had built their towers and whether they saved their cell phones or their children first. She wondered if there were others like her. But she didn't wonder for long, because then the pushing began in earnest and the baby was on its way. There was one last hot flash, much like the bang that started it 40 weeks back, a sensation so terrifically new, where she felt the sun, the earth, the water all around her, and the birth of this new world, too. She knew in that moment that she would call her baby Blue – if she were around to call her baby anything. With her last breath she connected with Blue, who blinked once with large knowing eyes and swam away.

Latitude adjustment: arrival in Stewart Island

Down South was always home, mint tea and my brother and me skipping stones in the creek out behind Papa's house, while Patti knitted sweaters for winters that never got too cold.

Now the world's on its head; *tea* is dinner and Papa is dead. Creek dry, house sold, and my brother and me skipping birthdays 'cause we feel old.

I bought a map and drove all over but I still don't know if I'll ever get used to looking right and shifting left, or finding the sun obliging us obliquely as she squats low, old and tired, to the North.

My birthday's tomorrow. Used to be we'd suck crab legs and chug Rolling Rocks. We were summer babies, Robbie and me; now I'm wearing extra socks and wishing my ma were here, but I know she won't come, she'd have to buy a new coat.

Now Down South means August cold snap, the forties roaring my wool cap off my head. This island's my home now, Ol' Stewart sees to it that I open my heart somehow and throw my anchor down, and stay. *Kia ora*, as they say.

No one dragged me here – sailed in and fell into more wilderness than I ever knew existed. But on my birthday I'll drink my usual bourbon and hear the ice in glasses, *tink-tink*, as I see my ma pour one more Julep from her cracked pottery jug, for me.

I'll smell the mint and hear Robbie's big-man laugh and wonder why he moved to Canada. I'll feel Papa's creek mud between my toes, I'll face east and feel the setting sun on my back and dream of going North.

Tell me what you think

"Dites-moi ce que vous en pensez," said the old woman. "Tell me what you think."

The girl had been gazing at the canvas, an astonishing explosion of colour amidst a grey background of tattered cardboard and greasy clothing and tired plastic bags, and she now sensed the woman's gaze on her. What could she say? That she wanted to press her cheek into the cool ocean purples, put her lips to the milky sky and drink? That the sweep of greens and browns rising up with the sun's golden fingers parting the trees just so hinted at the home she'd left and nearly forgotten? That the feathery texture of the grasses down low reminded her of the brush of her lover's hand on her neck, that she was sure that the depression in those tall wildflowers was made by him and her, right there. And that the line of black birds off in the distance placed a thin, cold emptiness in her chest which had nothing to do with the November Parisian morning?

For a moment, she wondered if she could take this woman around the corner and buy her a hot tea, sit with her and talk about the colour of warmth and love and home, of sorrow and loneliness and fear. She wanted to know how an old woman could capture everything that was in a girl's heart in such a small square. Instead, she tossed a coin into the woman's worn grey cap and muttered: "Oui, c'est bon."

Escalation

You…
and me.
You want to…?
Cool air, night yawning.
Pour me another, keep talking.
4am. Still here. Electric fingertips. Touch.
Your voice is music   between the sheets.
Dawn dapples your shoulder   I kiss the light.
I'll show you yours   if you show me   mine.
Don't fall to sleep. Tell me another story.   1001?   *Yes.*

A knobby thing

for John Wentworth Chapin

She reclines in her window seat, sees the starboard prop whirring super-fast, looking slo-mo. She closes her eyes and drifts back to yesterday, the last day of everything: 80-hour work weeks, devoted dull boyfriend, pet cat (a gift) she secretly hates. She brings her thumb to teeth, gnaws where there's nothing left to gnaw, sorrowful nails bitten down to nothing. She feels ragged but ready for anything.

The wheels touch down and she gathers her things, spits cuticle out the side of her mouth, *thp*.

She steps out into air so hot she's sure she'll never be able to breathe. The tropics. Then she inhales deeply and instead of feeling oxygen hitting lungs, she *tastes* it – floral and citrus, sweaty and sweet. The first breath is miraculous and jarring. She almost cries out; the punch of this new world hits her hard.

She wanders along the main street, spots the trademarked arches garish and gold against this landscape, jutting up amongst dusty buildings and peeling paint – an echo of her old world. She longs for the familiar cool, then spies a small market across the street.

Locals handle vegetables she's never seen or heard of.

She goes to the first long table piled with flowers and fruits, eyeballs a knobby thing, large and green. "Qu'est-ce que c'est?" she says timidly to the three women sitting in a circle.

"Breadfruit, love." The older woman, the one with droopy breasts and happy eyes, is the one to reply.

She picks it up, smiles. Thinks she'll give it a try.

Whale shark

She dreamed she was a whale shark dreaming she was a boy dreaming he was a whale shark dreaming she was a boy dreaming he was a whale shark dreaming she was a boy. Illuminating. Diving. Soaring. All in one night, or maybe it was one hour, or even one minute. She dove down down down and found fluorescent charms swinging from the snouts of seahorses. She flew firecrackerfast, fearsome and jubilant at the dizzying depths and the iridescent shape of things. She fed on plankton but they weren't plankton at all – they were morsels of delight, merry magical minstrels skipping on her tongue, pressing and lifting at the same time. Between bites (gapes, because there's no chewing when you're a whale shark) she napped and dreamed, and she was the boy, and she had a ladder, and she climbed and climbed and climbed. The ladder went up to the top of her house and beyond. It touched treetops and the salt of the sea-sky in the harbour. It exceeded the reach of her mother's call, way out in the everdark of the night. She dove through silk raindrops and she was a whale shark again, pectoral fin browsing slippery sand. And then she was a boy again. Shifting back and forth, down and up: first tail swish, long and smooth and elegant like a shark but not a shark, then boy with hands – hands! – digging a mote of water for protection (naturally) around a castle, singing sea-lavender songs. As a whale shark, she dreamed the boy, and as a boy, she dreamed the whale shark. And so on. Blueblack of ocean to blackblue of sky. Down and back up. Swimming laddering lunging climbing

She can be anything in her dreams.

She opens her mouth and swallows the stars.

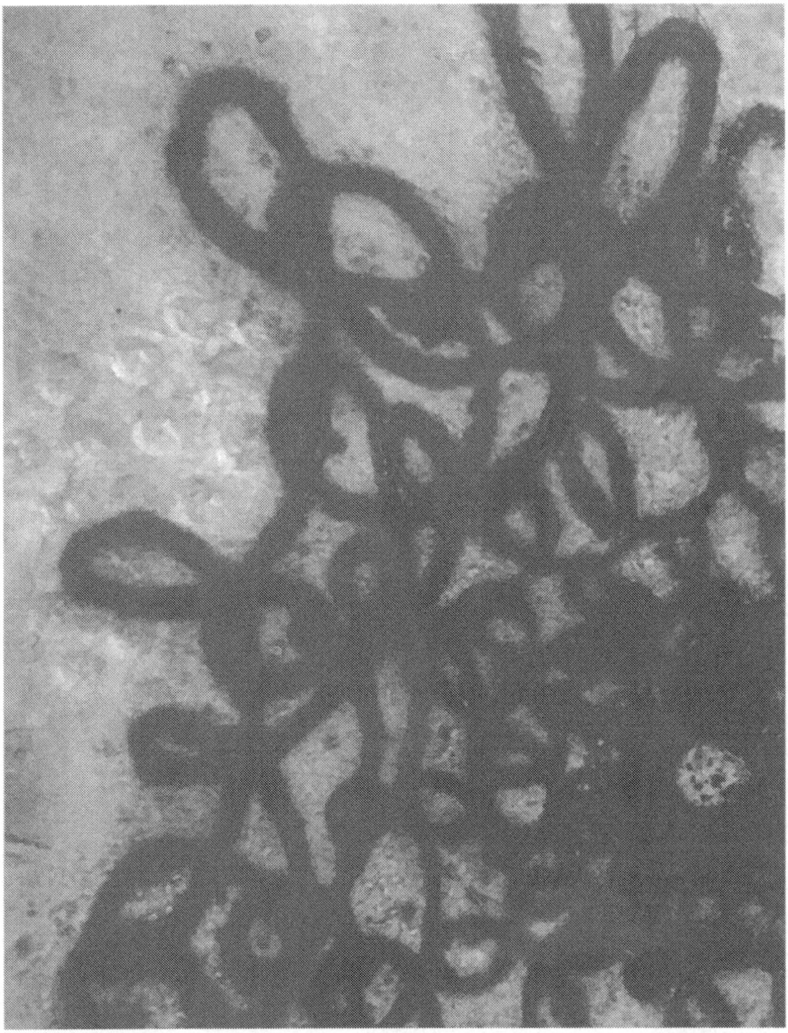

Acknowledgements

Deep gratitude to, and in memory of, Walter Bjorkman and Margaret Cahill. It was Walter who was there when I dreamed up Fuddy-Duddy (a decade ago), and who was in fact her one and only fan. Walt is also credited with writing the poem 'Kids!'. Margaret was a special friend and an intuitive reader / editor, someone with deep understanding of life and words on the page – and a marvellous feel for dry wit and humour.

Heartfelt thanks to:

Gail Ingram and Rachel Smith for the extra push, for fine-tuning and for being such excellent writing friends;

my daughters Lola and Jana for their eagle eyes, and their love of words;

Jennifer Halli for sharing her beautiful and inspiring artwork;

Jude and John at Ad Hoc Fiction for supporting my work – again! – and seeing this through to publication, with painstaking revisions and care;

Christopher Allen, Kathy Fish, Nod Ghosh, Tania Hershman, Erik Kennedy, Graeme Lay, Catherine McNamara, Paula Morris, Emma Neale, James Norcliffe,

Nuala O'Connor, Sam Rasnake, Ethel Rohan, Robert Scotellaro, Tracey Slaughter, Linda Wastila and Sian Williams for reading story drafts and supporting my writing over the years.

Thanks, also, to John Wentworth Chapin and the many creative spirits who were involved in *52|250 A Year of Flash*, the project that ignited a small but brightly burning flame, and to the writers in *Flash Frontier: An Adventure in Short Fiction*. Some of these stories appeared in those sites, in early versions.

Appreciation for the NZ Society of Authors and the Auckland Museum Library, who provided support in 2012. Some of this work was inspired by research during that year.

And, finally, grateful acknowledgement to the editors of the following publications where these stories and poems first appeared:

A-Minor Magazine: 'Aquinas, acid and me' and 'Longing'

Atlanta Review: 'The model bakery'

Bath Flash Fiction Award, and later included in *the everrumble*: 'Whale shark'

Blackmail Press: 'Lessons from childhood: watermelon' and 'apples' (in poetry form)

Blue Lyra Review: 'Black and white and grey'

BluePrint Review: 'Sled' (in collaboration with Walter Bjorkman, under the title 'Winter' and in slightly different form)

Drunken Boat: 'The Fuddy-Duddy Editor In The New Year' (in poem form)

Eastbourne: An Anthology: 'Pencarrow, now and then'

Headland: 'A midsummer night's shore'

Istanbul Literary Review: 'Close your eyes', 'Morning flash' and 'Time to rest'

Jellyfish Review: 'Fish forever'

JMWW: 'Snapper'

Landmarks: 'North'

Like Birds Lit: 'A knobby thing'

Manifesto: 101 Political Poems: 'The Wall: a love story, of sorts'

Metazen: 'Love, story' and 'Spin'

Microw: 'Wanderer'

New Micro: Exceptionally Short Fiction: 'And in the museum: triptych' and 'Antarctica'

Nivalis Short Story Anthology: 'Lost and found in Berlin'

Poets & Artists: 'Latitude adjustment' (in poem form)

Prime Number Magazine: 'X'

Ramshackle Review: 'Elephant'

Restore to Factory Settings: Bath Flash Fiction Volume Five: 'Roll the die'

Revolution John: 'Impossible weather'

SmokeLong Quarterly: 'Antarctica' and 'The Fuddy-Duddy Writer Looks For Her Story' in a different version called 'Why Flash: Five Vignettes'

The Airgonaut: 'Up the creek'

The Linnet's Wings: 'Itch' and 'Harmony'

Used Furniture Review: 'Lessons from childhood: the chair'

About the author

Michelle Elvy is a writer and editor who grew up on the shores of the Chesapeake and now makes her home in Ōtepoti Dunedin. She is founder of National Flash Fiction Day NZ and *Flash Frontier: An Adventure in Short Fiction*, and Reviews Editor of *Landfall*. Her anthology editing work includes *Bonsai: Best Small Stories from Aotearoa New Zealand* (2018), *Ko Aotearoa Tātou | We Are New Zealand* (2020) and the international *Best Small Fictions* series (since 2015). Most recently, she has been co-curating *Love in the Time of COVID: A Chronicle of a Pandemic*, with an anthology forthcoming. Michelle's poetry, fiction, creative nonfiction, essays and reviews have been widely published and anthologised. Her 2019 book, *the everrumble*, also published by Ad Hoc Fiction, is a small novel in small forms. This is her second collection.

michelleelvy.com

About the artist

Jennifer Halli was born in Pittsburgh, Pennsylvania and immigrated to New Zealand in 1998. Through ceramics and printmaking, Jennifer creates small-scale prints and large-scale installations that explore place and material while considering religion, loss and time. She earned an MFA in Artisanry from the University of Massachusetts | Dartmouth as a Distinguished Art Fellow and has practiced and worked with world-renowned artists from the USA, UK and Australia. Her experience and work have led to international exhibitions and artist residencies in Australia, Belgium, Denmark, Italy, Japan, Jersey, New Zealand and the USA.

Jennifer currently lives and works in Ngāmotu New Plymouth, Aotearoa New Zealand.

jenniferhalli.com

About the artwork

Winging
Collagraph print on Rives BFK
200 x 280mm

There is something significant about a move to a foreign country, especially when you are old enough to adopt it as home yet naïve enough for it to shape your character. As a young adult, I shifted to New Zealand with a desire or intention to find a less ordinary place.

I was surprised when *Winging* was selected as the cover for this book. It is a print and an oddity as I only printed the one. It is about contradictions and ambiguity and was made when I returned to the USA to work towards my Master of Fine Arts; I had not anticipated how difficult a return would be and found myself unsettled and foreign in my home country.

The print is a quick, almost temporal work with a I-have-nothing-to-lose attitude in the making – I was not only back in the USA, but in Missouri of all places. Through the exploration of abstraction, I was striving to capture a moment in the transition of life, of travel. The print is both grounded and airy, eager to drift to a better place but too weighty to do so. It is laden with potential; floating to a better place was in my thoughts at the time – with sights on landing back in New Zealand. Floating to what I view as 'the other side of better'.